LORRIE'S FIRST TERM

Norah Mylrea

ABBEY REWARDS
CRESTA HOUSE, LONDON

Contents

LORRIE'S FIRST TERM

CHAPTER I

How it all Began

The big room on the second floor of the Rectory at Combe Langley is called the Playroom when the younger children are in it—the Schoolroom when Miss Humphries and the three elder girls are at work—the Ironing-room when Nannie is working there with the week's washing to iron and mend—and, by the children themselves, the Glory-hole!

On this first of August, with the afternoon sun streaming in through the wide-flung windows, it was definitely the Glory-hole! Mary Grey, the eldest of the Rectory crowd, was patching a hole in her last year's gym slip so that her younger sister, Lorraine, could wear it again for the paper-chase on Saturday afternoon. Lorraine herself was still doing her preparation for Miss Humphries; Jacqueline was playing with Timothy in an attempt, she said, to keep him quiet, but as she was shouting even more loudly than he was, her efforts were not a brilliant success.

" For goodness' sake, do remember that this slip is thin all over, Lorrie," Mary said, holding up the gym slip to the light and viewing its threadbare condition with a doubtful eye. " If you squirm about as you usually do, it'll go through in the most awkward places."

" Oh, it'll do," Lorrie said cheerfully. " Last paper-chase I caught my shoulder on a bit of barbed wire, and split the thing from top to bottom! It turned out all right, though, 'cos I went in to Grannie Finch and she mended it for me, and gave me some home-made toffee to comfort me while she sewed! I know everyone is awfully sorry for us because we're so poverty-stricken, but actually I get rather a kick out of it."

" You wouldn't if you were Mummie, though," Jacqueline said, looking up from the house she was making with Timothy's bricks. " She worries so dreadfully about our not being able to go to boarding schools, and having no clothes and everything, the poor, sweet lamb," she finished, quite in Nannie's own tones.

Mary said nothing, but bent a little nearer her

sewing. It was all quite true, she thought miserably. Mummie was worried, and Daddy too, if it came to that, but Daddy seemed as if his faith lighted him up from inside like a warm flame— it irradiated the whole of his being, and the whole of his life, so that going without things just didn't matter to him. It didn't matter to Mummie either, personally, for so long as she had her children, and the Parish, and her garden, she was perfectly contented; but lately, as the three girls had approached grown-up-ness, she wanted so many more things for them—pretty clothes— boarding schools—holidays and all sorts of treats which she simply could not afford.

The Rectory was a big rambling house set in an old-world garden which, as a gardener could not be kept and the Rector was always so busy, was overgrown and wild, except for Mummie's "patch", as it was called, and here Mrs. Grey had managed to grow enough flowers for the vases in the lovely, shabby, comfy old drawing-room, and for the centre of the dining-room table. The rooms in the house were big and oddly shaped, so that although the furniture was shabby, they were still attractive; and if the cretonnes were faded and the rugs thin in the middle, no one noticed, for in the hearth in summer stood a huge brass bowl of lupins, and on the broad window ledges were great vases of delphiniums and larkspur.

There were five children at the Rectory—Mary, Lorraine, John, Jacqueline, and Timothy, a little fellow of five. The three girls were educated at home by Miss Humphries (known as " Honney "), and enough money had been scraped and saved from the family exchequer to send John to his father's old school at Winchester; but Mrs. Grey longed for good schools for Mary and Lorraine, who were old enough now to pass out of Miss Humphries' gentle care, and to take their places in a bigger and wider world. Lorrie hoped most passionately that the money would never be forthcoming for her to leave home and " pine away and die in some bleak seminary ", as she poetically put it; but Mary was studious and keen on learning, and although she would have hated saying good-bye to home, she often thought regretfully of the chances to study in peace, and of the wonderful teaching some of her friends were having, while she was still with " Honney ", who was a darling, but not a very brainy one!

" Who *did* write *The Essays of Elia*, Mary?" Lorrie asked, chewing the end of her pen thoughtfully. " Surely it was Holmes?"

" No, you're thinking of *The Autocrat of the Breakfast Table*," Mary said with a smile. " Hon-

ney asks us who wrote *Elia* every month or so;
I'd have thought you'd have known by now.
Lamb, you idiot."

"You needn't be so jolly superior about it,"
Lorrie said, hastily scribbling down the answer
as if, were she to wait another second, it would
have flown from her mind again. "Jackie,
go down and see if Nannie is making any scones
for tea, there's an angel, and if she isn't, be a bit
beguiling—yes, you can," as Jackie started to
protest. "You could wheedle the leg off a brass
monkey if you tried."

Nannie, who had been at the Rectory ever
since Mary was a baby, had now become house-
keeper and "bottle-washer-in-chief", as Lorrie
called her, and with a daily help, she and Mrs.
Grey did the work of the big old house between
them. The girls were useful too, and each had
her allotted household task, but Mrs. Grey
was against their working for more than an hour
a day in the house. She had come from a very
wealthy home herself, and she bitterly regretted
that her daughters should have to make beds,
wash dishes and sweep floors. The Rector, on
the other hand, thought that the household tasks
the girls did, did them no harm at all. Mary
agreed with him, but Lorrie and Jackie often
rebelled against their jobs, and thought that

when Mummie said, " I'm sorry, darling, that you have to work so hard," it was indeed a case for sorrow!

" Nannie says if Mary likes to make a few tea-cakes, we can have them, but she can't make them herself because she is too busy with the jam-making. There's some fresh raspberry jam, though, so I should think we could make that do." Jackie stood inelegantly on one leg and surveyed the room. " I wish she'd let me make some cakes, but she says I'm too extravagant, just because I used the best butter last time for those buns!"

" Well, if you want cakes, Lorrie Grey, you can jolly well go and make them," Mary said, not looking up from her darning. " It's to make you respectable that I'm doing this beastly thing, so it's up to you."

" I'll make 'em if Nannie will let me," Lorrie said cheerfully, putting her books in a heap on the little locker which was hers and served for a desk. " She's always a bit snorty with me, though, for no matter how fussy I am, the flour *will* spread itself all over the kitchen! Here goes, then, and if you smell a smell of burning, for goodness' sake come down. It'll be me doing King Alfred."

She ran down the narrow back staircase, and in a moment the other two girls heard her pleading

How it all Began

with Nannie, whose one remark seemed to be:
"Not all over my clean kitchen you don't, Miss
Lorrie."

In the drawing-room Mrs. Grey was lying on
the settee, doing the household accounts on an
odd scrap of paper with a short end of pencil—
and sighing over the enormous amount of butter,
milk, fruit and bread one seemed to need to
feed a family of eight people! The Rector
came in, just as she had made a note to "Ask
Nannie *why* ten packets of cornflakes in one
month!"

"Well, my darling, you look as if you had the
affairs of the world on your shoulders—what is
it? The month's books again?"

"Yes," Mrs. Grey said, putting them all away
and pocketing her scrap of paper. "We won't
talk about them now, though; it must be tea-
time. Is it my imagination or *is* there a frightful
smell of burning coming from the kitchen?"

"I hope it isn't a cake being burnt up," the
Rector said anxiously. "I forgot to tell you at
lunch-time, dear, but Miss Forsythe is about to
descend upon us! She met me in the village this
morning and said she'd pop in to see you this
afternoon. Yes, I know it's a shame, on my only
free afternoon, but what could I do about it?"

"You couldn't do anything, darling, but I *do*

wish she wouldn't interfere so. I try to keep my temper with her, because she is really awfully kind underneath that dominating manner, but it's very hard not to be rude to her when she will try to tell me how to bring up the children, look after you, and run the house! Considering she has thousands of pounds a year to live on, and only herself to think about, I'm sure I can't think why she considers herself a good judge of how we could manage on so little, and with such a huge family."

" Well, none of that matters a bit, since I know your difficulties and you know mine, and we have the most delightful family of children in the world, and a lovely old house, nice and shabby so that it doesn't matter how untidy we are, and we all love one another so dearly," he said contentedly; then, as a wail of anguish came from the kitchen regions, he strode to the door, opened it, and called: " What on earth is the matter, Lorrie?"

" Oh, Pops, my poor love, I had meant to make you such a lovely little cake, in the shape of a mitre—and now the beastly thing's collapsed and spread itself all over the oven shelf. Oh, all right, Nannie, don't fuss so. The old baking tin was nearly burnt through in any case."

There was the sound of grumbling from Nannie,

How it all Began

wails of anguish from Lorrie, accompanied by Jackie and Tim as they saw the precious cakes coming out of the oven like little pieces of coke.

Mrs. Grey and the Rector hurried to the scene, the Rector saying anxiously: "Well, someone must make some more cakes quickly. Miss Forsythe is coming, and there appears to be nothing for tea at all. Nannie, couldn't you make something nice in about ten minutes?"

"Not really, sir," said Nannie in the obstinate voice she always used when she thought she was being "put upon". "I've got this jam to finish, and everything," she ended rather lamely.

"Lorrie will stir the jam, while you make some dainty little sandwiches for tea, Nannie, please," Mrs. Grey said firmly; then picking up Tim and shooing Jackie out of the kitchen, she turned to Lorrie again and said: "For goodness' sake, pull yourself together, darling, and don't waste good eggs and flour by burning them. Aren't any of them eatable?"

Before Lorrie could answer, there came the sound of voices from the front door, and a second later Miss Forsythe, taking the privilege of a much older friend than she really was, walked straight into the house and through to the kitchen. Mrs. Grey flushed with displeasure, but the Rector said cheerfully: "Good afternoon, Miss

Forsythe. Here you see a domestic drama—Lorrie emulating King Alfred, and us watching the tea-cakes being thrown into the dustbin!"

"Oh, how distressing," she said in her high-pitched, rather affected voice. "But how very kind of Lorraine to try to make cakes—were they specially because I was coming to tea?" she asked coyly.

"Oh, of course," Lorrie said with a wicked gleam in her eye, for, of course, she had had no idea that anyone was expected. "I'm quite cast down now, Miss Forsythe, for I've burnt the lot." Then, to the horror of Mrs. Grey, she turned an innocent face towards the guest and said: "Won't *you* show me how to make some little tea-cakes? You are always *so* clever at everything."

Both her parents wondered if Miss Forsythe would realize the sarcasm of the remark, but apparently she did not, for she said in a delighted voice: "Oh, really, my dear child, that is *most* kind of you, but, of course, I'll show you." Then to the mutinous Nannie she said: "Now, Nannie, clear the table for us, and get me out some best butter—not that margarine—haven't you some dairy butter? Not used for cooking? How absurd! Really, my dear Ruth," she said, turning to Mrs. Grey, " it is *no* cheaper to use inferior foodstuffs. Now, Nannie, get me some currants, peel, sultanas, a lemon, some brown sugar, and some sweet almonds."

"Will you excuse me?" came Mrs. Grey's cold voice from the doorway. "I have some accounts to finish."

Miss Forsythe was far too busy ordering Nannie and Lorrie about to wonder where her hostess had disappeared to. In the drawing-room Mrs. Grey was pale with anger. "It's no use, Roger. I'll *have* to be rude to that woman, and as for Lorrie, she shall go to bed the very second we have the house to ourselves. Nannie will be in a temper for the rest of the week about this— and the whole month's groceries will be used up if that pair of idiots stay in the kitchen making their ridiculous cakes."

"What imp of mischief entered Lorrie to make her make such an asinine remark?" the Rector said, with a smile playing about his mouth. "That child was simply play-acting, for she is no more an admirer of Miss Forsythe than you are. Where, by the way, is Mary?"

"Upstairs sewing away at her old gym slip for that naughty little rascal in the kitchen," Mrs. Grey said grimly. "Instead of making up to Miss Forsythe, she should be doing her own mending. Just wait until I have ten minutes' private conversation with Miss Lorraine!"

Half an hour later, a very pleased and flattered Miss Forsythe entered the drawing-room. Close on her heels came Nannie, her face crimson with suppressed anger, and in her hands a tray laden with tea-things—including a small plate of little cakes, rather underdone-looking and quite flat.

"What a truly delightful child Lorraine is," Miss Forsythe said in a purry-purry-pussy-cat voice. "She was *so* grateful for the little instruction in cooking I was able to give her. Now, I wonder why you have never taught the girls to cook, Ruth, my dear? After all, as their mother, surely your first duty should be to instruct them in all household tasks?"

Upstairs in the Glory-hole Lorrie was giving a recital of the cake-making class, while Mary and Jackie rolled about with laughter.

"Oh, I wish you could have seen Nannie's face when Foxie-Forsythe made her leave her precious jam and wait upon her hand and foot! She simply stood there, me beside her looking as if butter wouldn't melt in my mouth, and ordered Nannie to bring this, carry that, wash-up the other, and be-quick-about-it! Nannie kept shooting the *filthiest* glances at me, and all I said was: 'Yes, Miss Forsythe, and no, Miss Forsythe, and oh, how clever!' I tell you it was as good as a play. Mummie retired in high dudgeon, and

How it all Began

I bet I'll have to answer for my sins, but oh, heavens, it was well worth it! And if you could see the measly little plate of cakes at the end of it!" And she rolled over again with laughter.

Tea in the Glory-hole was a hilarious affair, for Lorrie kept remembering more details of the cake-making, so that when after tea she was sent for by the Rector, she was still giggling, although trying very hard to look both innocent and repentant!

In the drawing-room the Rector was alone—standing by the window, facing the hearth, where Lorrie, knowing she was " on the mat " for her sins, remained standing looking at him. She was amazed to find his usually gay face rather grave, and to notice in his eyes a serious expression which she had not expected. She had known he would inflict some mild punishment on her for having caused her mother some annoyance—but here he was looking quite severe.

" I'm not Daddy at the moment," he said, reverting to an old custom of the family. " I'm the Rector, and you, Lorrie, are a little girl who has not played the game quite fairly."

" Oh, darling, I don't think you can say that. I was only joking when I said Miss Forsythe could do everything—I'd no idea she'd take me at my word."

"Then you had no ulterior motive when you made up to her like that?"

"What *is* an ulterior motive, exactly?"

"Some other reason—some way of getting personal gain."

Lorrie looked at him with a hurt expression clouding her eyes. "Oh, Pops, you know I wouldn't 'suck up to her'," she said. "And anyway, what could I get out of her? You know I don't like the interfering old thing."

"Don't speak like that, please, my dear," the Rector said seriously. "The truth is that Miss Forsythe has made a very splendid offer to us on your behalf, and I understood from what she said, that she had already broached the subject to you and Mary. Don't say anything just for a moment, but go and ask Mary to come down, and I will go and find Mummie, and we'll have a family conference. Anyway, my darling, I'm sure you did not behave so naughtily this afternoon with any other idea in your bad little head than having fun." He pulled her towards him and kissed her.

She ran up to the Glory-hole, where Mary was reading and Jackie was dancing to the ancient gramophone, while Tim was having his play-hour with Nannie.

"Come down a minute to the drawing-room, will you, Mary," she said rather breathlessly.

How it all Began

Mary put down her book and got up, while Jackie said: " What's up? You look as if you'd had a shock. Daddy wasn't the Rector when you got down there, was he?"

" As a matter of fact, he *was*," Lorrie said. " You could have knocked me down with the proverbial feather! I don't know what Miss Foxie has been up to, but I've never seen Daddy so Rectorish before. Come on, Mary. There is a family conference on."

The two girls could see at a glance that something of importance had happened to worry their mother—although she did not look altogether displeased. " Mary, what did Miss Forsythe say to you after church on Sunday morning?" she asked, as the two girls seated themselves side by side in the window-seat.

" Oh, just general things, I think," Mary said, wrinkling her nose up thoughtfully. " Something about that horrible niece of hers—Prunella —and about the school she goes to. She asked me if I didn't envy Prunella, and then she asked that idiot of a Lorrie, who said . . ." She could not finish what it was Lorrie had said, for giggling.

" Don't let us worry about what Lorrie said, for the moment—just try to remember what you said."

" Oh, I was rather angry After all, Mummie

darling, it doesn't help people to rub it in about their not being able to go to expensive schools like Devenham. She is always the same. She says, ' What a pity you can't travel a little, it's *so* broadening for the mind,' and then goes on about how Prunella went with the Fourth form to Brittany last year, and hopes to go to Paris when she is a little older."

" Yes, dear, I see all that, but you still haven't said what answer you gave to Miss Forsythe when she asked you if you did not want to go to school."

" Well, she said, ' Don't you envy my niece going to Devenham,' and so I said, ' No, I jolly well don't. I'd rather stay at the Rectory, just as we are.' "

" Oh, so that is what you said," the Rector put in kindly, then added in a quiet tone: " And would you truly rather stay than go to Devenham?"

" Not really, because I'd love to go to a big school—but as we can't afford it, I don't see any reason to bemoan my fate to people like Foxie."

" And now, what did you say, Lorrie, when she asked you?"

" Oh, I cast my eyes up into her face, and I put on a funny voice and I said, ' Oh, Miss Forsythe, I'd *adore* it,'—you know, in the same sort of affected tone her horrible niece uses! Then Mary and I got the giggles, so I asked her to excuse us, as we were quite overcome at the mere suggestion of going to the same school as Prunella."

The two girls watched while their parents exchanged glances—then suddenly Mary exclaimed: " Oh, darlings, don't tell me she means to pay for us to go—it would be altogether too, too rapturous!"

"Would it indeed?" Lorrie said indignantly. " I'd hate it, nothing would induce me to go, especially if Foxie paid. I'd hate to be under an obligation to her, she'd always be reminding me of it."

" Lorrie, dear, don't be unchristian," the Rector said. " If Miss Forsythe wants to be kind and wants to help you, you should do your share and be grateful."

" But is it true?" Mary said. Her face had gone quite white and her voice was tense. " It's the thing I've always longed for and dreamed of. Honney is a darling, but I do think I've got a bit beyond her now. Oh, Mummie darling, why are you looking like that?"

" It isn't you Miss Forsythe offers to send, sweetheart," she said sorrowfully. " It's that naughty little Lorrie. I did my best to make her change, but she said she had spoken to you both, and knew quite well which of you deserved the treat. While you were upstairs mending Lorrie's frock, Lorrie was unwittingly playing into Miss Forsythe's hands—and as Miss Forsythe has no sense of humour, she took all Lorrie's nonsense quite seriously."

" Oh, how unfair it is," said poor Mary, the tears coming to her eyes. " I'm sorry," she said, sniffing. " I ought not to have said that. I'm awfully glad for you, Lorrie."

" Well, I'm not, and I'm not going, and that's all about it."

" I'm proud of the way you took your disappointment, Mary," the Rector said, putting an arm round her shoulders and drawing her to him. " As for you, you bad little lass, you'll do as Mummie and I think best."

" It's Basseton I'm worried about," murmured Mrs. Grey softly. The Rector said quietly: " Oh, don't worry about that. I don't suppose the girls go anywhere near it."

Lorrie wondered what Basseton was, but was too full of her own thoughts to inquire. It seemed the most awful mistake in the world that she, and not the studious Mary, should be given this opportunity—Mary, who would have worked so hard and done so well!

" Run along now, darlings," Mrs. Grey said. " Nothing is finally fixed up, so there is no need

to bother your heads about it until Daddy and
I have talked things over and decided what is
best to be done."

Upstairs in the Glory-hole Mary threw herself
down on the old sofa and burst into tears, saying
between her sobs: " Don't take any notice of me,
Lorrie, I'm a fool, but it's much better to howl
and get it over than try to bottle it all up inside
me."

" I won't go, I promise you," Lorrie said
miserably, looking in amazement at Mary's tear-
stained face, for Mary was the self-controlled one,
and never except once, when Mummie was ill,
had Lorrie seen her cry.

" Oh, but you must," Mary said, sitting up
and dabbing at her swollen eyes. " You must go
and made a great success of it. I'm a selfish,
egotistical, beastly sister, that's what I am—but
oh dear, I would love to go."

" I suppose it's very ungrateful and all that,"
Lorrie said savagely, " but I wish Miss Foxie
Forsythe had never been born or thought of,
coming here where we were all so happy, and
interfering and breaking up our lovely lives. Oh,
why was I ever such an idiot as to play up to her?—
and now the laugh's on me!"

CHAPTER II

Last Days at Home

During the days which followed, the subject of Lorrie's departure for school was, by common consent, not referred to. Mary, to all outward appearances, had forgotten the incident of Miss Forsythe's offer, and went through the daily round of little tasks as if nothing had happened. Only Lorrie knew how, after the light was out in their bedroom at night, Mary smothered her tears in the pillow, and wished again and again that some fairy-godmother would materialize— wave her wand, and produce enough money for Mary to go to boarding school.

On Lorrie's conscience, like a heavy weight, pressed the thought that, by making fun of Miss Forsythe, she had robbed Mary of her great chance. For certain it was that, if Miss Forsythe really did want to benefit one of the Rectory children, Mary was the most suitable as well as the most deserving of them all. By getting on with her household tasks, poor Mary had left free the field for Lorrie, bent on mischief to "play up to" Miss Forsythe, and this one prank, and her mock serious answer on the previous Sunday, had procured for Lorrie a boon which she was far from seeking—and had stolen from Mary the great chance she had always longed for.

Jackie, having been asked by her mother not to talk about the plan to either of her sisters, maintained a moody silence, for she thought it would be awful to lose Mary's help in lessons— to lose Lorrie as a companion and a fellow-conspirator was an unbearable thought!

John, who was still on holiday, and had been out fishing with the squire's son on the memorable afternoon of Miss Forsythe's visit, had been told the news that night, after the girls were in bed. He knew how hard it was for his parents to send him to Winchester, and also guessed how difficult it was for Mary never to complain when all the extra money was spent on him—while she stayed on, still having lessons with Honney! He adored Mary, and was furious that this chance should have come to Lorrie who, in his opinion, was "feather-brained" beside her more serious sister. Still, he agreed with his mother that, though the great chance was open to Lorrie alone, it would be wrong to refuse it.

"Who knows?" said the Rector with a tender

smile. " Our ' bad hat ' may turn into a ' blue stocking ' yet!"

Mrs. Grey winced at the mixed metaphor, and gave it as her opinion that school for Lorrie would certainly tame her down a bit, which was a thing greatly to be desired.

In due course came a letter via Miss Forsythe, from the Head of Devenham, saying that Lorrie could be received there as a boarder—and that the new term commenced on the 21st of September. It enclosed a list of things she would have to have, and at the length of the list Mrs. Grey shuddered rather!

The time had come when yet a further family council would have to meet, and the sooner the whole thing was discussed, agreed upon, and received as a settled fact, the better it would be for them all, she felt. She went upstairs to the Glory-hole, expecting to find the girls still at their lessons, but remembered that Honney had suggested a botany ramble to be followed by a picnic-tea down in the water meadows. The afternoon was golden with sunshine, and a thousand scents rose up from the herbaceous borders beneath the Glory-hole window. Mrs. Grey decided that her news would be better received out of doors than in, so started off towards the water meadows and down to a favourite glade where, as she expected, she found her family.

Mary and Lorrie were unloading the picnic-baskets, while John, higher up the stream, was fishing one moment and paddling with Timothy the next. Jackie, whose knowledge of botany was practically non-existent, was being instructed by Honney in the clover field the other side of the hedge.

"Darling, what brings you here?" Mary cried, dropping a loaf on to the grass and coming towards her mother. "I hope you've brought another cup, sweetheart, and mean to stay to tea!"

"She can have my cup," Lorrie said, hanging on to her mother's other arm. "It's lovely to see you, darling. Why didn't you tell us at lunch-time that you'd come down?" Then, cupping her hands to her mouth, she shouted through them to John to "See who's here."

It gave Mrs. Grey a delightful warm feeling round her heart to see how quickly John dropped his rod, caught up Timothy in his arms, and came racing through the meadows towards her; and to see Jackie climbing the gate; and to feel the tremendous gladness of the two elder girls at her arrival. "What a pity," she thought, "that for Mary, at least, I bring disappointment—and for Lorrie the certain knowledge that these lovely days must come to an end and she must leave us all."

They settled down to buns and milk, with tea for Honney, Mrs. Grey and John, and rusks for Timothy. It was not until it had been cleared away again that Mrs. Grey handed the Devenham letter to Lorrie, and told Mary to read it too. She noted the flush of mortification that overspread Mary's cheeks, and saw her set her jaw, in determination not to let her feelings show too much.

Lorrie said emphatically: "You know I don't want to go to the wretched school, darling. Surely there is some way of getting out of it?"

"Don't be an idiot," John said, going over and sitting beside Mary, as if he knew that by being near her he was a comfort to her. "You're hopelessly backward, I should say, and here is a chance to get on a bit. Surely you mean to do something for your living later on! Well, you won't get very far if you know no more than you do now," he ended, with brotherly frankness.

"I'm not so backward as you make out," flared Lorrie; "and in any case I mean to take over old Cook's field and have a poultry farm—and a thorough knowledge of French verbs isn't absolutely necessary for that, I hope you'll agree."

Last Days at Home

" No, but if you forget to feed your chickens in the same way that you forget to learn your French verbs, they'll all die, and that'll be the end of you, as well as the end of them, poor things," Honney put in.

" Yes, that is certainly true, but this is beside the point," Mrs. Grey said. " Both Daddy and I think that it is a pity the offer is not open to Mary, but since it isn't, we feel that you should take it, and do your level best to justify Miss Forsythe's kindness to you."

If the news had come to Mary, she would have been too overcome by all that it meant to have spoken. But Lorrie was scanning the list of things Matron had said she would require, and was giggling over the extent of it.

" Four pairs of outdoor shoes, one pair of gym shoes, one pair of bedroom slippers," she read aloud.

Jackie said inelegantly: " Golly, why four pairs of outdoor shoes? It sounds dreadfully extravagant."

" You should worry," Lorrie grinned; " as I'll have grown out of 'em by the end of the first term, they'll all become yours! Glory, girls, we shan't know ourselves. By the way, Mummie darling, does Foxie pay for all these things?"

" Don't use that horrid nickname," her mother

said reprovingly. " No, of course Miss Forsythe isn't paying for all your clothes—it is more than kind of her to pay your school bills."

Mary said seriously: " It'll cost a lot to get her all these things, won't it? Surely some of her clothes will do—her winter coat is practically new, but it's brown—and it says here a ' Navy Blue Reefer cloth coat '. Perhaps we could have her own coat dyed!"

John said hastily: " Oh no, Mary, don't suggest that. It's horrid going with poor kit to a new school." Then he flushed, for he saw the pained look on his mother's face, and realized too late that he had disclosed something which he had always hidden from his parents. He added quickly: " Not that I know anything about it personally, of course—but I've known boys come to school . . ."

" I know it's been difficult for you, darling," Mrs. Grey said sympathetically.

" Well, you needn't worry about me," Lorrie said cheerfully. " If they don't like my clothes they can do the other thing. Prunella Forsythe is bound to be an unpleasant little snob in any case. How old was she when she came down to stay last?"

Mrs. Grey said she thought the child had been seven, but as that was six or seven years ago, it

Last Days at Home

was stupid of Lorrie to imagine she was still a nasty little girl.

" She was more than just a nasty little girl," John said grimly. " She was a sneaking, deceitful, conceited little cat!"

Mary and her mother " went into a huddle ", as Lorrie put it, over the list, and the rest ran back to their own occupations. Lorrie went down to the river to wash the plates, and there sat looking into the tree-shadowed water, wondering what life at a big school would be like. She wondered, if when she got there she found it unendurable, the family would greet her with open arms when she came home—having run away!

The long winter days would soon commence, she thought. The end of September usually saw them still in the woods and fields for picnics and rambles. But October and November meant long evenings by the fire in the Glory-hole, and stories told by firelight—and secrets about Christmas presents, and little visits to Salisbury—the nearest town—to buy really good presents for Mummie and Daddy. Ah, well, she'd be home for the Christmas holidays, that was one thing—home in time to help to dress the tree for the village children, and perhaps, this year, as a real school-girl, Daddy would allow her to help to decorate the church for Christmas!

(P777)

No use, she thought wisely, to look for trouble before it actually came, and perhaps she'd find she loved school. How beastly, though, that Mary couldn't come too. She spent a few idle moments thinking how wonderful it would have been if money had been plentiful, and both she and Mary were being taken up to London to be " kitted-up " with clothes. How joyful they would have been over all their new things. But now an enormous effort would have to be made to find money for all those items on the list—and all the time Mary would be thinking, " If this were only me ".

This, of course, was what Mary, sitting on the bank beside her mother, was thinking at the same moment, but with the thought was the pride she felt in the friendship she had with her mother. She felt that both her parents had confidence in her, and found her a great help in their many worries over the family.

" Then you think you can darn her white sweater to make it fit for hockey?" Mrs. Grey said, ticking off the item on the list.

" Yes, and perhaps Honney could undo her navy blue jumpers and knit them up again with the school colours at the neck and cuffs," Mary said thoughtfully.

. . . .

Last Days at Home

At The Grange, Miss Forsythe was reading a letter which had come by the afternoon's post. It was from her niece, Prunella, and it said:

"DEAREST AUNTIE,

"I was amazed by your news that Lorraine was to come to Devenham as your protégée next term. Of course, I think it's awfully Christianlike of you to pay for her, especially as I remember her as being such a tomboy and no good at lessons. I remember I had lessons with the Rectory children and their ghastly governess, Honney, when I stayed with you one summer, and Lorraine was awfully backward then, and took no pains with her work at all. She may have changed now, though. I only hope when she comes to school she won't be dressed in the awful clothes those children used to wear, and that she won't be too pious and priggish! When I was there it used to be the regular thing for Lorraine to inherit all Mary's last-year's clothes, and for Honney to undo all their jumpers and knit the worn-out wool up again! I don't say we're ultra-smart at Devenham, but, thank heaven, we aren't quite as poor as church mice!

"Your loving niece,

"PRUNELLA."

CHAPTER III

Lorrie Sets Out

The long hot August days seemed to Lorrie to fly on enchanted wings. Never could she remember days turning into weeks and weeks into months as quickly as these August days turned into the first crisp days of early September.

To a girl who had never had more than one new garment at a time, the outfit she was now having made for her seemed enormous. Mrs. Wibben, from the village, was set to making undies—while Miss Fips, who was considered in Combe Langley as being a modiste of the highest rank, came and measured Lorrie for her school dresses, which, according to Matron's list, should all be bought at some expensive West End store, but which Miss Fips declared she could make equally well, and at a third of the price.

Mary was being splendid. Never for one moment did she allow her envy to make her tongue sharper—or to slow down her knitting needles, as they flashed through the white wool of a gym sweater. She had mercifully one great compensation against disappointment—she was

allowed for the first time to practise on the church
organ. She was very musical, and this was the
one thing that, in those last days before Lorrie's
departure, seemed able to comfort her.

At last the 21st arrived! The girls were up at
sunrise, for there still seemed a thousand things to
do to complete Lorrie's kit. Her train to London
left Salisbury at 10.30, and there was the long ride
in the doctor's ancient car before one got to
Salisbury from Combe Langley. The Rector did
not boast a car, but old Dr. Green was always
ready to lend his Morris, which, although it was
ten years old, yet managed to cover the roads
comfortably and get one to one's destination without more than a few splutters under its old-
fashioned bonnet.

Mrs. Grey and Mary were to go to London
with Lorrie, and put her in the care of Miss
Heywood, the Third-form mistress, who was in
charge of all the London girls.

Lorrie, feeling suddenly most awfully tearful,
looked out from the window of the Glory-hole,
over the fields and away down to the water
meadows where all her life she had played. The
little village lay still, as if it had not yet wakened
from its sleep, but over towards the church spire
a column of smoke rose from old Grannie Finch's
cottage, and cut the view in half—the sleepy

cottages on one side and the brook and meadows on the other. Suddenly an inspiration seized Lorrie, and she ran down the back stairs and out into the fresh dewy air, across the Rectory garden, and through the little wicket-gate into the churchyard.

The old Norman church was never locked, for the Rector believed that the House of God should be open to His children by day or night— and in all his years of ministry, no one had ever taken advantage of his faith in humanity.

Lorrie had never been in church quite so early before, and she was impressed anew by the lovely feeling of peace which came to her as she knelt by the altar rails and asked God to help her in her new life—to comfort and reward Mary— and to bring her home safely at the end of her first term. She rose with a new feeling of confidence and hope. It seemed to her as if the inner voice, which we all may hear if we sit in quietness and faith, had told her that, come what may, she would triumph if she kept the light of her faith undimmed and her courage undaunted.

At breakfast Timothy demanded to know why everyone was so quiet. " Has Lorrie been a bad girl, Mummie?" he asked, seeing how quiet his usually noisy sister was this morning.

" No, darling. She is being good and brave,

and she is setting out on a lovely adventure, and
we are all wishing that we might go along with
her. But she'll come marching home again soon,
to tell us all her news. We'll sit round the fire in
the gloaming, and she'll tell us all about the girls
and the mistresses and what fun it all is."

Going up in the train was a great adventure in
itself to the two girls, for money was too scarce
at the Rectory for holidays, and it was seldom
that they went away from home. The Rector,
whose duty it always was to take John back to
Winchester, had pressed Mrs. Grey's hand in
ready sympathy as he said good-bye, for it is
difficult for parents to part with their children,
and to have to face the fact that their babies are
growing up.

They had lunch in town, and then went on to
Waterloo, where, as soon as they got near Platform
8, they heard jolly voices, and saw a crowd of
schoolgirls, all wearing navy-blue coats and navy
berets with the school crest worked on the front
of them. Miss Heywood, tall and thin, came
towards them and said in a clipped, cold sort of
voice: " Are you Mrs. Grey?"

Mummie said yes, she was. They shook
hands, then Miss Heywood turned to Lorrie
what that young lady secretly thought of as a
" fishy " eye!

Lorrie's First Term

"You are a bigger girl than I expected," she said, as if Lorrie's tall slim figure were her own fault entirely. "Come along, I'll introduce you to your fellow-travellers."

"I'd better leave you now, my darling," Mrs. Grey said, knowing that if she stayed any longer she would not make a very brave show of saying good-bye.

Mary stood looking along the platform to where a studious-looking girl of her own age was seated on some trunks, her head buried in a book, as if the surrounding bustle and noise had no effect on her. How wonderful to be going off into this new world of books and learning! Ah, well, there was her precious music and her lovely home, and if having these, she still complained, she deserved to be spanked, she told herself.

Lorrie was clinging to her mother in a final hug. She threw herself then into Mary's arms and gulped something about, "I wish this were you instead of me," then dashed off down the platform, almost cannoning into the rigid back of Miss Heywood.

Without another look back, Mrs. Grey took Mary's arm and they hurried away.

"This is one of the new girls," Miss Heywood said to nobody in particular. The girls all smiled encouragingly, and one dark-eyed girl came forward and drew Lorrie into a group, whispering as she went: " Don't take any notice of ' Hey Nonnie, Nonnie ', she's always so beastly dreary. What's your name, old thing? Mine's June Martin."

" I'm Lorraine Grey—called Lorrie for short," she said, feeling better already for the friendly welcome. " I've never been to school before, and I'm scared stiff."

" Nothing to be scared about," June said cheerfully. " It's always frightful going back after being at home, but after the first day or two it gets less sore, and in a week or so you're in the thick of hockey matches and exams, and no time to think of your troubles until term is over, and you're back again in the bosom of your family. Going home, especially for Christmas, is heavenly."

" Yes, I can well believe that," Lorrie sighed regretfully, feeling that she had never appreciated her home and family half enough.

" All in now, girls, please," Miss Heywood said, shooing them forward as if they were a flock of sheep. There were three reserved compartments for the Devenham girls, and Lorrie, sticking closely to June Martin, managed to get into the first one with her and eight other girls as well. They seemed a laughing, jolly crowd, and Lorrie wondered how they could possibly be so happy when leaving their homes and their parents. The train slid from the platform. In the next compartment Miss Heywood's voice could be heard warning the younger girls with whom she was travelling to keep away from the open windows—not to make so much noise—to sit still, and a dozen other orders, all, it seemed to Lorrie, in one breath.

" Listen to ' Nonnie No '," a girl called Sally said, with a jerk of her head towards the next compartment. " Thank goodness we've reached the age when we don't have to travel with her. She used to infuriate me when I was small."

" Have you never been to school before?"

" Never. I don't want to go now, either. I'm the victim of a kindly deed—if you can imagine anything so dreadful."

" Do tell us," June urged, for she had taken to the new girl at once, and liked the candid expression in her wide-set eyes, and the fact that, unlike most new girls, she seemed prepared to talk without bragging!.

So Lorrie, whom the family had always accused of " liking an audience ", launched forth into an account of Miss Forsythe's sudden charitableness —and went on to Mary's cleverness and the awful mistake Fate had made in sending her instead of Mary to Devenham.

June, listening, thought that Fate was far wiser than Lorrie believed, for it was just this type of girl that the school wanted.

" I expect you'll be in the Fourth with us," Sally Garnet said, looking wise. " You'll escape Miss Heywood then—she teaches the Third-form kids. We call her ' Hey Nonnie, Nonnie No ' —the Hey, because of her name, and the *no* because it is her favourite word! She is probably well-meaning inside her shell, but her shell is so thick and hard that nobody ever seems to pierce it!"

" Don't distress the poor young thing," June said with a giggle. " It may happen that she will *be* with Nonnie No, then see how you'll have prejudiced her, on her very first day, too."

" Oh no, she'll be certain to be in the Fourth at least. How old are you, Lorrie?"

" Nearly fourteen," she answered, but already her spirits had begun to wilt as she remembered how she had always slacked at lessons, and what a poor opinion Honney had always had of her. How dreadful if she were put in a form with quite little girls—and under this appalling Miss Heywood!

As the train pulled into Devenham Station,

the mistress leaned from her carriage window and began issuing orders right and left.

"No girl is to attempt to leave the carriage until I open the door for her myself. Get in there, Marjorie. Sybil, if I see you leaning from that window again, you may take an order mark. Now"—as the train stopped—"come along, children," she said, marshalling her own carriage companions on to the platform and lining them up into a crocodile. She opened the other two carriage doors, and at last the girls were allowed to troop out.

Lorrie had expected a school bus to meet them, but June told her the school was only ten minutes' walk across the fields, and as the day was fine, the bus wouldn't be coming for them. Like a sergeant-major, Miss Heywood marched the girls from the station across the road, through a turnstile, and so off across a footpath to the back entrance of Devenham.

Lorrie, knowing that her first impressions would remain with her all her life, looked at the great grey stone buildings of the school with eager eyes. Once within the grounds, the girls were allowed to fall out of their lines, and Lorrie, following the crowd, went round the buildings, and so into the enormous quadrangle in front of the school. Here the turf lay like a billiard table—

so smooth and close-cropped. Three tall elms shaded the lawn with their red-gold autumn leaves. There was a high wall beyond which enclosed the entire school, save where great iron gates opened from the main drive to the road.

It was a far bigger, grander place than Lorrie had dreamed of—no wonder, she thought, that Prunella Forsythe was so proud of being a Devenham girl.

At the thought of Prunella she ran and caught up with June, and said breathlessly: "By the way, do you know Prunella Forsythe?"

She knew that her people would expect her to be especially nice to the niece of the woman who was doing her such a great kindness. She had disliked Prunella very much that summer when she had come to the Rectory to do lessons with them, but now she was older, pray heaven she was less snobbish and patronizing. June's reply, however, did not sound as if any great change had been worked in Prunella by her life at school.

"Do I know the Prune? I'll say I do. Horrid example of English girlhood, don't you think?"

Before Lorrie had time to answer, Prunella, looking much older and, if possible, more superior than ever, sauntered across the greensward towards them.

"Well, Lorraine," she said, shaking hands in

a very grown-up way, " I should have known you anywhere. You haven't changed a bit—still the same amusing creature I remember you used to be."

" Now, some people could have said that, and I'd have liked it," thought Lorrie, " but I certainly don't like it from Prunella."

" Yes, we neither of us have altered much," she said, trying not to sound as if she thought a little change in Prunella would be an advantage.

" Oh, so you've met in the good old days," June put in. " How nice for you, Lorrie, having an old friend to show you around. Deal gently with her, Prune," she said, with a grin at the furious look on Prunella's face at her hated nickname.

" I, and my family, are certainly dealing gently with the Rectory crowd," she said bitingly. " As I am sure Lorrie will tell you, *she* has no cause to complain of my people's generosity."

" Golly, you sound like a benevolent society. Come on, Lorrie, or the Prune will be tipping us a shilling!"

As they walked away, Lorrie was conscious of the venomous look Prunella darted at her. She was not to know until later that Prunella had always longed to be taken up by June Martin and her crowd, but had so far been kept out because of her patronizing airs and her snobbery. She watched Lorrie, arm in arm with June, being greeted by Sallie Garnet and Clare Martell, and she felt herself grow cold with rage. That wretched Rectory kid, whose people never had tuppence to their names, coming here by the charity of Aunt Florence, and walking away on her first day with the jolliest and most popular girls in the school! It was maddening, and she wasn't going to stand for it. She'd jolly soon show Lorraine Grey where her place was, if it meant telling the whole school that Lorrie had come here out of the charity of Prunella's aunt.

Meanwhile, Lorrie was being taken round the school by June and Sally. Devenham was once the home of a foreign ambassador, and the main entrance and hall had been left as they were then, but two long wings had been thrown out from the main building, and the whole place scientifically turned from a mansion into an up-to-date school. June opened the door of a large room filled with rows of desks, with a raised dais at the end, under the big open windows. " This is the Fourth-form chamber of horrors," she said. Then, taking Lorrie by the arm again, she led her down a passage until they came to a big room where, it seemed to Lorrie, hundreds of girls were sitting, standing or lying—talking at the tops of their voices.

"No need to tell you that this is the Middle School's common-room," June shouted above the din. "The Third, Fourth and Upper-Fourth live here—the Lower School has its own c.r., while the superior Fifth and Mat. forms have studies, lucky blighters."

Actually there were about forty girls in the common-room, but as they never stood still for a moment, they managed to make themselves look like a vast crowd.

A tall, fair-haired, serious-looking Senior came in just as June was introducing Lorrie to some of the girls, and at her entrance June whispered: "This is Honour Stevenson. She is to be Head Girl this year. She's marvellous—we've all got a 'rave' on her."

Certainly the Head Girl's entrance had silenced the babel, except for the welcome they gave her in much softer voices than they had been using a second before.

"Hullo, Honour, glad to be back?"

"Marvellous to see you again, Honour. Had a good time?"

"Come to tell us to be good girls this term, Honour?" This, of course, from June.

Honour smiled. "Yes, I have come to tell you

to be good. You get told that every term, it
seems to me, but you still remain the same unruly
crowd of ruffians."

There were cries of " Oh, no—that's unfair,"
and " Nobody could accuse *me* of being unruly."

" Anyway, girls," Honour said solemnly, " it
isn't up to me to preach to you—the Head
will probably do that in chapel to-night. All
I want to say is that I hope you'll keep up the
fine traditions of the school. I want you to be
especially kind to the newcomers, and remember
what you felt like in your first term, and try to
make them feel at home and cheery. Sally Garnet,
you are Sports Captain for Lower School, aren't
you? Well, try to run things as well as Priscilla
Davis did last year and you'll do. Olive Bradley,
you won the Prefects' Vote last term, so you are
the Prefect for the Upper Fourth. Clare Martell,
you are the Fourth's Prefect, and you, Pamela
Brown, are Prefect for the Third. Now, girls,
remember that you voted and selected your
Prefects for yourselves—stand by them—help
them in what I can assure you is a hard task—
and don't let them have to appeal to me to punish
any of you. There will be a Prefects' meeting in
my study after prayers to-night."

After this long speech, she went quietly out
of the room. There was an instantaneous out-

burst of talking again. Clare Martell was seized by June and waltzed round the room.

" Fancy my own bosom friend being lauded and honoured above me, and set on a pedestal and worshipped from afar! And now we shall have to say: ' Yes, Clare ' and ' No, Clare ', and ' Please, Clare ', and ' Oh, Clare '. Come along, Miss Prefect Clare Martell, pray give us your views on the modern schoolgirl and her disgraceful manners!"

" Now, my good girl," Clare said threateningly, " you'll forget we were ever nursery playmates, and treat me with the proper respect due to a Prefect—or—take a thousand lines!"

There was a scuffle at this, which ended in the two girls rolling over and over on the floor. Lorrie gazed down at them in amusement, and was sorry when, as a bell rang loudly through the school, they had to get up and fly to their dormitories to prepare for tea.

The long dormitory was divided off into ten cubicles, and Lorrie was rather surprised when she saw her own name pinned on the blue curtains of one of them. Inside was a bed covered with a blue coverlet, a blue-painted dressing-table, blue chair, and blue bedside table. Everything was in miniature, so that although the cubicle was not very large, there was yet plenty of room to move about

in it. Over the bed was a lovely picture of the
Madonna, wearing a blue cloak, and as all the
blues in the room exactly toned with the beautiful
Madonna blue of the picture, the cubicle looked
both artistic and inviting. Instantly Lorrie loved
it. She had never had a room of her very own
before. At the Rectory she had always had to
share with Mary. She looked round her small
domain now with great pride, thought of her
small collection of books and wondered if she
could save her meagre pocket-money, buy a little
bookshelf, and paint it blue to tone with the rest.
She tidied her hair, then went along to the dormitory bathroom, where the entire Fourth was
washing its hands and talking—the scrimmage
round the washbasins was amazing.

Tea was a plain but wholly satisfying meal of
brown bread and butter and buns. Lorrie found
herself seated with June on one side—and, alack!
Prunella on the other. That young lady complained about what she was pleased to call the
" hateful food ", and held forth about the cream
cakes, éclairs and brandy-snaps she had been
eating " this time yesterday " at home. June said
witheringly: " No wonder you're a mass of
spots, old girl, if that's the sort of thing you eat.
You'd better not let Sally hear you grousing
because you can't have a lot of sickly food, or

she'll make you run ten miles every day, to clear your system of poisons!"

" I am not as sport-crazy as the rest of the school, thank heaven," Prunella said with dignity.

After tea the girls went in to chapel, a lovely consecrated little church lying in a quiet meadow below the school. Here, for the first time, Lorrie saw the Head and heard her voice.

Miss Graham's voice was perhaps her most noticeable as well as her most attractive characteristic. It was a lovely voice, beautifully modulated, clear and resonant. As she read the Collect for the day, Lorrie thought she had never heard the wonderful words so inspiringly spoken, and thought, with a sudden smarting of her eyes, of how the Rector would have enjoyed such good reading.

The Head was tall and slim, with dark hair and grave dark eyes. She was an impressive person, but such was the quality of her voice, that Lorrie felt instinctively that though she would respect her, she would never be afraid to go to her in trouble.

As Honour had predicted, the Head " preached them a sermon ", which was really a heart-to-heart talk to inspire them to try harder, work more diligently, and play, with free minds, conscious of work well done and leisure earned. She pointed out that good behaviour need not mean dullness—on the contrary, she said, if one has behaved well, one is happy and carefree—a good companion in the truest sense of the word.

After supper, Lorrie, with three more new girls, went down to the Head's room, and she spoke to them, each in turn alone. While she waited for the first girl to come from the room, Lorrie wondered if she dared ask the Head which form she was to be in, because she felt if she were not in the Fourth, she would be utterly cast down. She had no way of finding out how high the standard at Devenham was—all she had to go on was Honney's rather pessimistic forecast that she would never be up to the standard of girls of her age if she didn't work hard. Well, she told herself, she would certainly work hard at Devenham *if* she were in the same form as June and Sally, but if she were put down in the Third, under the icy Miss Heywood, she'd " pine away and die ".

" Your turn now," the new girl said, coming into the hall from the Head's room. Her face looked flushed, and Lorrie said anxiously: " Not an awful ordeal, was it?"

" No worse than I deserved, I expect," she answered. " I'm a lazy idiot, I know, and now it seems I'm to receive the benefit of all my wasted hours!"

"Oh dear," Lorrie sighed dismally. "I'm in the same boat as you, then! Ah, well, here goes," and, tapping at the door and hearing the quiet "Come in," she marched boldly inside.

"You are Lorraine Grey? My dear, I hope you are going to like us all," were the Head's utterly unexpected words. Lorrie shook hands, and murmured something about being sure she would *love* them all—which she thought was rather an exaggeration if Miss Heywood were an example.

"As you haven't been to school before, I shall have to give you a test paper to-morrow, and then decide from that which form you are to be in. I hope you will justify my putting you in the Fourth, as that is the form for girls of your age, but if I have to put you in the Third for a term you mustn't be disappointed, because it will be so much wiser for you to get a good grounding than to try to do work beyond your standard. Did you see the girl who went out just before you?"

Lorrie said she had

"That was Judy Grenville, a new girl and about your age. She has been to a day-school until this term, and she brought with her her last terminal examination paper. It was not very well-marked, so I have had to put her in the Third form. If you have to go there—and I am rather afraid, from your mother's letter, that you will— you will have her as a companion in distress!"

She went on to say that she hoped Lorrie would be happy, but Lorrie was in despair. She knew before she sat for the test paper that she was doomed for the Third, and nothing Miss Graham could say could make up for her disappointment in not being with June and Sally.

She went to her cubicle, after a jolly time in the c.r. with the rest of the girls, and looked again at its sunny-coloured walls and its delphinium-painted furniture, and thought, in an effort to cheer herself: " Well, at least I shall have this sanctuary to come to, whatever misery the day may have brought."

From farther down the dormitory came June's gay laughter, then Prunella's voice asking her to " for heaven's sake go to sleep and stop that horrible din."

" Are you all right, Lorrie?" called Rosemary Burton, dormitory prefect.

" Oh yes," Lorrie said, slipping between the sheets and snuggling down. " I love my cubicle."

" Your cubicle! How do you know it's yours yet? If you get turfed out into the Third form, my good girl, you'll not have a cube to yourself," came Prunella's sneering voice.

Lorrie's First Term

" Oh, surely I won't have to give this up?"

" If you are put in the Third you will, old thing," June said; then added in a reassuring tone: "You won't be in the Third, though. The Head sets very easy papers for new girls, and you're our age, so this is about right for you. Don't let the Prune discourage you; she's our professional wet blanket—gifted above all others for dampening the brightest spirits!"

But Lorrie lay, long after the others were asleep, thinking of Judy Grenville, who certainly *was* in the Third in spite of her age, and who had looked so mournful as she left the Head's study.

"Back at the Rectory now," mused Lorrie, " Mummie and Daddy are sitting by the fire in the drawing-room, with the french doors open on to the moonlit garden, and they are imagining me asleep—and happy. How awful to have to write and tell them that I am down with girls much younger than myself—and oh, how awful to have to leave this dear little cubicle—and June and Sally."

Tears of self-pity and home-sickness fell down her cheeks, and she had to turn on her face and bury it in the pillows, so that any other wakeful person should not hear her crying.

CHAPTER IV

The Third Form for Lorrie

Next day, as she finished the last of the four
test papers, she felt that her worst fears were
realized!   The questions, which at her first
anxious glance had not seemed so bad, were on
closer inspection much deeper, and required
much more actual knowledge of facts than Honney's ever had. At the Rectory, she reflected dismally, she had always been able to " bluff " her
way through—with a grain of knowledge and a
peck of imagination.   But the Head's set of
questions required facts—and those facts, alas,
she had either never learned, or, having half-
learned them, had entirely forgotten.

She had sat with two other girls in the common-
room for the test. One girl, a studious, rather
priggish creature, remarked that she thought the
questions too easy—rather a disgrace, she felt,
if one couldn't answer them at the age of thirteen.
The other girl giggled at this, said she thought
she might have " scraped through by the skin of

her teeth ", and left it at that. Only Lorrie was certain of failure.

Her mood of intense depression was printed on her face as she went into the dining-hall for mid-day dinner, so that it was unfortunate that the first person she should meet should be Prunella, looking perky and, Lorrie thought, unpleasantly triumphant.

" Well, how is the Rector's little daughter getting on?" she asked, a slow smile curving her thin lips. " If your famous Honney is anything like she was that summer I had lessons with you, I should think you'll be in the kindergarten!"

" That would be preferable to being put next to you in form, if you still cheat as you did that summer. Remember when your answers and Mary's were so alike that Honney moved Mary, and asked you to do the sums again—and the second time they were all wrong?"

" That's not true," Prunella blazed, her thin face going white with rage. " Say that in front of any of the girls, and I'll tell them you are here on charity. I suppose your father went round cadging to Aunt Florence, as vicars always do."

Lorrie waited for no more. Her temper had always been her biggest burden, and now, to hear her beloved father spoken of so slightingly filled her with rage. She flew at Prunella, and forced her back against the wall, raining blows on her with clenched fists. This was the scene that Honour Stevenson, with three or four more Seniors, encountered as they came in from the quad. Prunella broke away, and stood panting and gasping, her hands pressed over her heart.

" What, in the name of all that's undignified, is this?" Honour said in a freezing tone. " This isn't like you, Prunella."

By this time most of the other girls had arrived, and a crowd stood round, viewing the scene with lively interest.

" I was asking Lorraine Grey whether she had done well in her entrance test. She thought she ought to have done better, I suppose, and something I said seems to have driven her crazy. She rushed at me like a mad bull. She was always like that as a child, though—the whole village thought she was mental."

" That is enough," blazed Honour. " You ought to be thoroughly ashamed of yourself, Prunella Forsythe. You have been here for years, and you are the only girl Lorraine knows, and instead of helping her you seem to take a fiendish delight in tormenting her. What exactly did she say to you, Lorraine, to make you behave so abominably?"

" I shan't repeat it," Lorrie said, dusting her

frock with a hand that shook, and making feeble attempts to look less dishevelled.

"Yes, I should think silence is best. You will write a hundred lines for me by Wednesday, and I should think they had better be, ' I must remember that a lady does not fight '." There was a general titter at this, and Lorrie felt more foolish than ever. Prunella joined in the laughter, but Honour swung round and said cuttingly: "As for you, Prunella, I can't give you lines, as you are in the Fourth, but I can and *do* give you an order mark, and you can tell Miss Carrol that it was given because I found you fighting a new girl in the dining-hall."

So already Honour knew that she was not destined for the Fourth, thought Lorrie miserably, as she took her seat beside June—was it possible that the test papers were already marked, or had the Head told Honour that she was afraid she would have to put Lorraine Grey down with the younger girls?

It was so unlike Lorrie to worry about anything as she was worrying about this form question. She felt that by being so backward, she had given Prunella a chance to be condescending and overbearing. So far she had not met any of the Third form girls, except the new girl last night, and felt sure she would not—could not, in fact, like any of them as well as she liked June and Sally.

June said, turning to her: "Good for you, Lorrie. It's the first time I've ever seen the Prune look scared;" then turning to Prunella: "You *were* scared, weren't you?"

"I was amazed," Prunella said in a grown-up tone. "I knew the Rectory crowd were pretty crude, but I did think they stopped at behaviour of that kind—the way Lorraine flew at me was so very reminiscent of Billingsgate."

"Now what on earth does all that mean?" June said in honest surprise. "I must tell you, Lorrie, that our Prune, whatever her faults, has a most astonishing flow of highbrow words, which she lets forth every now and then, and fills us with admiration!"

Well, one thing at least could be said for Prunella, thought Lorrie, she isn't sulking as much as one would have thought.

"How you ever managed to get away from the Rectory alive, Prune, must be one of the Seven Wonders," Sally put in, still grinning at the thought of the "rough house" they had just witnessed. "I'm going to be frightfully nice to Lorrie after this—I didn't like the professional way she hit out with her right, and followed it up with a left swing!"

The whole table was laughing over the incident, and to Lorrie's surprise, Prunella joined in—made quite an amusing anecdote of how outraged she had been when she saw Lorrie's fist coming dangerously near her nose—and altogether behaved with such good sportsmanship that Lorrie wondered if she had misjudged her.

As they trooped out from hall and into the warm air of the late September afternoon, she managed to get near to Prunella. She had gone over and over in her mind what was to be her attitude towards this girl, and she had decided that whatever it would be in future, she would try to make a fresh start now.

"I'm sorry, Prunella," she said quietly, expecting Prunella to turn and accept her apology in the same spirit as she had accepted the laughter of the dining-hall. Instead, Prunella looked at her with disdain, did not stop, and threw over her shoulder: "I should think you would be. You'll be sorrier still before I'm done with you."

"What an odd mixture the wretched girl is," Lorrie mused, walking alone beneath the trees. She had not enough experience to know that many people are one thing in public, and something quite different in private. Prunella had never been a popular girl at Devenham, but she was ambitious to get into a jolly set—to be one

of the girls in the Fourth who stood out among
her friends as being amusing and a good sport.
She had hated it last night when Lorrie, by
doing nothing at all to gain favour, had been
accepted by June and Sally as one of themselves,
when, after years at school with them, they still
treated Prunella as a mere acquaintance. She had
hit back at Lorrie when that person's fists had
come for her, but she knew before she started
that she was quite unable to thrash Lorrie as
she would have liked to thrash her. During
Honour's interruption she had gone quickly over
her plan of campaign, and had decided that, whatever she did to revenge herself on Lorrie, she
must appear sporting to the form—she must make
light of the whole affair, so that afterwards people
remembering it would think Lorrie the sulky one,
and Prunella the sport who had made a joke of
it, and been prepared to laugh at herself as well
as at her opponent.

All this was beyond Lorrie's understanding.
She was an open, honest, unsuspecting soul,
and she just could not understand why it was
that Prunella could be so amusing and jolly at
one moment—and so utterly beastly the next.

As she had feared, the result of the test was
pinned on the notice board, and June, having seen
it immediately after dinner, came out to find

her and to break the news as gently as possible.

" Awful shame, Jack Dempsey," she said, pretending to be afraid of Lorrie, and ducking every time she raised her hand. " Don't hit me for six if I tell you the news—you're in the Third. It may not be as bad as you think though, because in brackets the Head has written ' for the present ', so if you are a good little girl and work hard, and say, ' Every day in every way I'm getting gooder and gooder ', you may, in a month or two, aspire to the Fourth, and be with really brilliant people, like Sally and me!" she ended with a grin.

" Oh, June, I'm sick about this," Lorrie said dismally. " It wouldn't matter if Daddy were well off and paying for me, but it'll be hateful having to write and tell Miss Forsythe that I'm such a dud. I bet the Prune will write it all most joyously."

" Now listen to me, Lorrie," June said seriously. " You haven't had the same chances as the Prune (or any of us, if it comes to that). I came here when I was ten and I'm nearly fourteen now, so you see I've had years of good grounding and regular work. It's no good looking miserable about your place in form; the only thing to do is to hurry up and come out of the Third, and you can do that quite well if you work hard. Make up your mind you'll be a Fourth-former next term,

The Third Form for Lorrie

and resign yourself to the Third for this. You won't like Hey Nonnie No much, I fear, but she's a marvellous teacher—and her lessons and lectures are some of the best we get. If she finds you are working hard she'll unbend a bit, and you'll find she isn't such a terror as she seems at first."

"It's you and Sally I'm regretting most," Lorrie said, though already she was feeling comforted by June's words and her own resolution to make good.

"We'll have wonderful times together, just the same as if you were in our form Try to get into the hockey eleven, and for goodness' sake take an interest in sport. That's one of the things the Prune is a fool about; she is not only slack at sports, she's openly contemptuous of them, and that at an English school is the unforgivable thing."

Lorrie went down to afternoon school feeling dreadfully shy and self-conscious. Miss Heywood greeted her with: "Ah, Lorraine Grey! Well, I hope you will work hard and get yourself into the Fourth by end of term. You had better sit at the desk next to Judy Grenville, who is about your age and is also new. For the time being you had better share books until your own are ordered."

Lorrie's First Term

The afternoon dragged by. The lessons were certainly interesting, but they were almost as far beyond Lorrie as the test papers had been. She tried so hard to concentrate that by four o'clock she felt utterly weary. Judy linked arms with her and they went in to tea together. It was sickening to find even her table changed, and afterwards, when she went to change her shoes, she found that her things had all been moved from the little blue cubicle and were now in the long Third-form dormitory.

If she had seen the Third dormitory first, before she had lost her heart to that little cubicle with the blue curtains and the view over the fields down to the river, she would have thought what a pleasant place it was. Now she viewed its pale-pink walls and rows of pink beds with angry eyes —it all seemed so very babyish after the cubicles— as if wherever she went she was to be reminded of her own backwardness, and the fact that, had she worked harder at home, she would have escaped these indignities. If only it had been Mary here, instead of herself! Mary would have had a cubicle, and a good place in the Fourth. She would have been welcomed with open arms by the Head, for she would quickly have discovered Mary's scholarship and love of learning. Instead, Foxie had insisted upon the "dud" of the family being sent to a school where she would never shine as a pupil, and where, because of her bad start, she felt she would never be really happy.

As she made these morbid reflections, Judy came swinging down the dormitory, humming a tune and apparently without a care in the world. "Topping dormitory, isn't it?" she said cheerily. "I slept in a cubicle in the kindergarten last night. It was meant for a junior mistress, I believe, but as the Head hadn't quite decided where I was to go, they put me in there. It was very quiet, because the kids go to bed at half-past six, but, my goodness, it was like Bedlam early this morning! You ought to have heard them—like a nest of young birds, all chattering at once."

Lorrie wondered if Judy herself were chattering to put her at her ease. She said, still nursing a grievance: "I was in the Fourth last night, in a lovely cubicle. I'd hoped I'd stay there. I hate a dormitory—no privacy or anything," she ended lamely.

"What are you two doing up here?" They turned and saw a girl coming towards them, smiling cheerfully, but shaking a finger at them. "You're not allowed to stay up here, you know. I'm Gay Campbell, Sports Captain of the Third, and very much at your service. I've been hunting for you everywhere. We're organizing a hare-and-hounds run for this evening, and we hope you'll join in."

"Oh, rather," they both said, and followed her downstairs to where, under the trees, the rest of the form were collected, spinning a coin for hares.

"Wait a shake," Gay called, breaking into a run as she saw the penny spin in the air. "It's no good deciding anything until we've seen what Lorrie and Judy can do. Now you two, double up, and sprint down to the cycle shed and back, and let's see what you're made of."

Lorrie went to bed that night worn out by a marvellous run as one of the Third-form hares. Her one achievement had always been running, and now it had stood her in good stead. She had easily beaten Judy in the run to the shed and back, had won the toss, and had started off with Gay as a hare. They had gone across the big field at the back of Devenham, hugged the hedge by the river, doubled back for half a mile, and stopped to rest by a hayrick within three miles of the school gates. They had seen the pack coming when it was several fields away, and had loped gently back to school, definitely the victors of the chase.

If all the Third were as sporting and friendly

as Gay and Judy, she thought, thankfully climbing into bed, she wouldn't mind nearly so much as she had thought. If only Miss Forsythe hadn't to be considered, and if only the Prune hadn't forced her into a bad beginning!

" Are you comfy there?" Kitty Lambert, dormitory prefect, called as soon as " lights out " had sounded.

Lorrie assured her that she was, and in less than five minutes she was asleep.

CHAPTER V

A Gating!

The days flew by on studious wings. Lorrie, full of determination to do well and become a Fourth-former by next term, had never worked so hard before. Miss Heywood, who prided herself on being able to read a girl's character almost on sight, had to admit to herself that in the case of Lorraine Grey she had been mistaken. When she had first seen Lorrie swinging along the platform at Waterloo with a swagger which, had she been a more thorough student of human nature, she would have understood as being mere bluff put up to cover an embarrassing moment, she had thought, " Ah, here we have another little wild animal," which was her way of thinking of girls who were more interested in having fun than in work. Actually, of course, she was right. What she didn't know was that, for the first time in her care-free life, Lorrie was " up against it " and meant to win through.

She had not seen much of June and Sally

because their time-tables were different. They
had had one or two jolly evenings when, prep
finished and supper over, they had met in the
common-room for singing or playing round
games. Prunella never missed an opportunity,
at these times, of saying something which rankled
in Lorrie's mind for days afterwards—but she
never said or did openly anything unpleasant, so
that the girls had all forgotten the fact that
Lorrie and the Prune were sworn enemies.

Lorrie, owing to her success in the " hare-and-
hounds " chase on her first evening, had been put
in the second eleven for hockey, and was showing
such good progress that Gay Campbell had told
her she had a hope of being in the first eleven
before the inter-house match in November. This,
apart from her determination to do well in the
terminal exam, was the one ambition of her life
now, and she worked hard and played hard too,
and wrote home glowing accounts of life at
Devenham.

Mary wrote every week, as well as Mummie
and Daddy. She told Lorrie of all the little happenings at Combe Langley, only omitting the fact
that she read Lorrie's letters about school with
such envy in her heart that she now took them
to bed with her to read, so that the rest of the
family should not see how they upset her. " Foxie

is rather impossible, these days," she wrote. "Because she is paying your school fees, she thinks it gives her the right to boss Mummie about—it makes my blood boil. She told Daddy that Prunella had said your test papers would have disgraced a child of six—but as Daddy *knew* Prunella would never have been allowed to even *see* your papers, he soon squashed that."

Judy Grenville was a grand friend to have, Lorrie soon realized. Her people were in the Far East, and she was absolutely alone in England except for an elderly aunt with whom she spent the holidays. She tried hard not to grumble, she said, and always wrote cheery letters to her people, but as she couldn't go East until she was eighteen, the future was not very rosy. Her aunt was old-fashioned and difficult, a great believer in keeping young people in what she was pleased to consider their "place", which, Judy said with a bleak look, was either in the schoolroom—or in bed!

It was fun on half-days to have an hour on the practice field, to rush away and change, and then with Judy and Gay to go down "town" and spend their weekly shilling on tea and toast at the Yellow Lantern—a café which specialized in good substantial teas for the Devenham girls.

On Wednesday afternoon it poured with rain, and Gay said it was no use hanging about hoping

A Gating!

they could play hockey, because the field was a mere puddle. In the common-room Sally and June were reading, having "bagged" the best chairs by the fire; the rest of the Fourth were either reading or playing Lexicon, while the Third girls, finding most of the games already "bagged", walked aimlessly about, grumbling at the weather, the Fourth-formers, and everything in general.

"I love walking in the rain," Gay said, and looked around for a kindred spirit. June looked up from her book and said: "If you're only doing a mile or so, I'll come along too."

Prunella, sitting alone in the window-seat, looked at the grey heavens, thought how unutterably dreary a walk in the rain would be, but was so keen on "getting in" with June that she said: "Oh, I'll come too, if I may."

A term ago June would have said yes at once, but the thought of the Prune's beastliness to Lorrie made her hesitate a moment. Prunella noticed the pause, and said viciously: "Oh, don't bother, I never go where I'm not wanted."

"Don't be a prize ass," June said, instantly ashamed for not being more gracious. "Of course we want you. I was amazed to think you'd like coming; I always thought you hated any form of exercise."

But Prunella was on her high horse, and, after arguing with her for a few moments, the two girls started. Lorrie, meanwhile, had been in the form-room, working on an imposition Miss Heywood had given her for carelessness. As the girls passed the form-room she came out, and June thought she looked rather tired and languid. Quite forgetting Prunella, she said enthusiastically: " Come on, old girl, get your ' mac '; we're going for a walk in the silvery showers."

" Oh, how wizard!" Lorrie exclaimed, remembering how often the Rectory crowd walked through the woods at Down End while the soft, warm rain trickled through the leaves on them. " I haven't quite finished that impot of Nonny's, though. I can do it before school to-morrow morning. Hang on a shake, June, and I'll be with you."

So it was that Prunella, nursing her grievance as usual, looked out of the window and saw June and Gay waiting in the porch, and the next moment saw Lorrie, still half in and half out of her mac, hurry out and join them. The three girls linked arms and went gaily off, leaving Prunella simply livid with rage.

She told herself that Lorrie's coming had ruined any hopes she ever had of June's friendship. She persuaded herself that but for Lorrie, she and June would be bosom friends. She quite forgot that in nearly four years of school life she had not achieved her object—no, it was all Lorrie's fault. She was welcomed with open arms, while Prunella was given to understand that her company was not wanted.

"I'll bet she has said hateful things about me to June," she told herself savagely, remembering how Honney had discovered that she had cheated all that time ago. "I was only a little kid," she excused herself. "Small children often do that kind of thing." In her heart she knew that Lorrie would never repeat her accusation to the other girls, but it pleased her wounded pride to tell herself that the Rectory crowd had always been hateful—hateful and altogether beastly.

Judy Grenville, waiting for Lorrie to come from the form-room, sauntered up to Prunella and began to talk. The Prune said with outward good nature: "How is it you aren't out with your friend Lorraine this afternoon?"

"The silly idiot made a careless mistake in her translation this morning, and Nonnie No gave her the whole of it to do again this afternoon—so she is in the form-room doing it."

For a second Prunella wondered if she should say, "Oh no, she isn't, she's gone off with June," and so make Judy angry that Lorrie hadn't been more loyal to her. But on second thoughts she realized that Judy was not like that, and would be the first to see that if Lorrie were asked by a Fourth-former, she couldn't drag anyone else along too.

But after Judy had gone, she wondered if she could possibly use her information. She felt sure that Lorrie had left the translation unfinished, for it was then only half-past two and there had not been time to do it since dinner. She started off to the form-room, intending to go through Lorrie's desk and find out if the translation were finished or not, but before she arrived there she met Miss Heywood hurrying along the corridor. " Oh, Miss Heywood," she exclaimed with a smile, " have you seen Lorrie Grey anywhere? I wanted her to lend me a book."

" She has an imposition to do for me," Miss Heywood said, turning back and opening the form-room door as she added: " I expect she is still at work on it."

Of course the form-room was empty. With hidden glee Prunella saw the suspicious expression that crossed Miss Heywood's face. She said tersely: " Lorraine doesn't appear to be here. You had better look for her in the common-room."

Prunella went off, knowing only too well from past experience that Miss Heywood would go

A Gating!

through Lorrie's desk until she found the imposition—and if it were not done, woe betide her!

Back in the common-room Prunella curled
herself up on the window-seat again with a book,
to await events. She had not long to wait. In
about five minutes Miss Heywood, with a lowering
countenance, stood in the common-room door
and asked if Lorraine Grey were there.

"No," Judy Grenville said, "she is still doing
her imposition, Miss Heywood."

"Unfortunately she is doing nothing of the
sort. Come, girls, surely some of you know where
she is."

"I think she went out with June Martin and
Gay," a Third-former said in a small voice. "I
thought I heard her voice from the quad."

Meanwhile, little thinking of the trouble
brewing for her, Lorrie was eating hot buttered
toast and sipping tea with all the delight of one
set suddenly free. Gay was telling them about a
tea-party she had had at home, and June was
joining in every now and then with a contented
grunt. It was lovely in the Yellow Lantern. A
big wood fire danced and crackled in the old-
fashioned fireplace, and people kept coming in
out of the rain, and ordering tea, and standing
warming themselves by the cheerful blaze, and
making everything jolly and homelike.

Lorrie's First Term

" It's the Head's birthday, some time this term. We always have a most marvellous party, or, if the weather is lovely and mellow as it sometimes is in late October, we have a picnic in Fourteen Acre Woods," Gay told Lorrie. " It's the one high light of the term, until the Christmas play and the match with the Fourth just before breaking-up."

" I believe the party is about now," June said thoughtfully. " Anyway, it must be within the next two weeks. Oh, I *do* hope the weather holds good. It would be hateful if it turned out a day like this, because a picnic is always miles more fun than a party."

Lorrie thought so too. They paid their bill and, still laughing and chatting, made their way through the rain-sodden lanes back to Devenham.

It was not until after prayers that evening that Miss Heywood sent for Lorrie. She was in her study, and, thought the culprit, looking like a thundercloud! " And may I ask where you have been all this afternoon?" she inquired coldly.

" I went down to the Yellow Lantern and had tea with June and Gay." ·

" *After* you had finished the imposition I gave you?"

" Well, no. I hadn't quite finished. I meant to work at it before breakfast to-morrow morning."

A Gating!

"And so break another school rule," Nonnie No said bitingly. "I think it is time that you understood that at Devenham we do not allow girls to do their work when and how it pleases them. Your translation this morning showed great carelessness—it might have been the work of a Second-form girl rather than that of a girl who should be in the Fourth."

Lorrie felt the colour flooding her cheeks. It was a sore point with her that she had been put down with girls younger than herself. She felt her temper rising, but tried hard to control it by studying the pattern of the carpet. This seemed to infuriate Miss Heywood, who went on:

"I should have thought the disgrace of being with such young girls would have made you more careful, but no—you do careless work, and then, when another chance is given you, you leave it to go gadding down town with girls of your own age who have the brains to get into their appropriate forms."

"I've been working fearfully hard," Lorrie said, trying not to let her voice break.

"And so I should think. You have a great deal of back laziness to make up for. I shall expect the imposition by to-morrow afternoon— you can finish it during mid-morning break. Understand that work before breakfast is *not* allowed. For disobeying the rule and going out when you should have been working, you will be gated next Wednesday and you will have an imposition given you. You may go."

"What a filthy temper she must be in," Judy said as Lorrie repeated this conversation to her in the dormitory. "I can't think why she went looking for you. I quite thought you were in the form-room, until she came bouncing into the c.r., full of vengeance!"

"I'd no idea she'd take it so seriously," Lorrie said morosely. "I don't care much, because I've spent all my pocket-money this week, and I want to start saving from now on for Christmas presents, so staying in and working won't worry me."

"What did Nonnie No want you for so badly, Lorrie?" Prunella said next morning. "She was searching the school for you."

"She wanted to gate me next Wednesday," Lorrie said tersely. "I just slipped down town for tea without quite finishing an impot she'd given me—I knew I could get it done by the morning, but she found out I'd gone, somehow."

"I really do think that as you are here on charity, you might make some attempt to obey the rules, and not try to dodge your work so abominably."

A Gating!

"Oh, shut up and mind your own business!"
Lorrie flashed. "Anyone would think *you* were
paying for me."

"So I am, indirectly," Prunella said. Then
added viciously: "Pity you're gated *next* Wednesday, though, as it happens to be the Head's
birthday, and we're all going for a picnic."

Lorrie, thinking it all over, wondered if it were
possible that Miss Heywood had forgotten that
the picnic would be on that day. She talked it
all over with Judy, who was thoroughly miserable at the thought of going to the woods without
her. Had she told June or Gay about it, they, as
older members of the school, would have advised
Lorrie to go to Miss Heywood and ask if the
gating could be postponed until the next half-
day; but Lorrie, although she thought of this,
was too proud to humble herself before anyone
she disliked so much as Miss Heywood, so that
although she viewed the preparations for the picnic
with misty eyes, she refused to ask favours, and
made up her mind to stay behind when the others
all went off to enjoy themselves.

CHAPTER VI

She Plays Truant

That was a dreadfully dreary week for Lorrie!
It was bad enough to hear the girls all so en-
thusiastic about the picnic, and to see the weather
getting better and better every day—to realize
that Wednesday would probably be a golden day,
with little fleecy clouds against a blue sky, and
autumn tints in the woods and a red-gold carpet
of leaves at their feet. Miss Heywood grew more
and more exacting about Lorrie's work, although
the rest of the form seemed to get off fairly lightly.
In the common-room Prunella was like a mosquito,
always buzzing about ready to sting. It amused
Lorrie to know that the Prune obviously thought
that the fact that she was there by the charity
of her aunt was unknown to June and the rest—
whereas, of course, Lorrie had spoken of it quite
openly the first day of term. One of the ways the
Prune had of trying to hurt Lorrie was to hint
that the other girls would " cold-shoulder " her
if they knew how poor the Rectory crowd were—
and she was annoyed when Lorrie only smiled

and said: "Thank heaven the rest of the form are not as disgustingly snobbish as you are, my poor Prune."

Lorrie looked forward to her home letters that week as a weary man in the desert looks forward to an oasis! But when they came they only plunged her into deeper gloom, for Timothy had caught a severe chill, and old Dr. Green was now afraid it might develop into pneumonia! She could tell by the forced cheerfulness of her mother's letter that she was dreadfully worried about Tim, and poor Lorrie longed again to be home with them all so that she could be on the spot to hear the latest news.

She did not feel she could confide in anyone, so nursed her troubles in silence, going about with a worried frown between her usually laughing eyes, and, as Prunella said spitefully, as if she were the only person in the world who had been gated on a half-day!

On Sunday, as they walked to church through the fields, Judy said seriously: "Can't you tell me what's wrong, Lorrie?"

"I can't begin to tell you," she answered mournfully. "Everything in the whole wretched world is wrong. Nonnie No hates the sight of me—and I certainly return the compliment. I'm sick of hearing about the lovely time you are all going to have next Wednesday, and added to that, I've had a dreary letter from home. If that isn't enough misery for one person to have to bear, I'd like to know what is."

"Well, it's no good brooding over it. Perhaps you'll feel better after church."

"No, I shan't," Lorrie said, getting more bitter the more she contemplated her woes. "Church always reminds me of home—and I don't want to start longing for home; it will only make me feel more miserable than I do already, if that's possible. I wish I could think of some way of dodging church this morning; I'm in no mood for it."

Judy had never known Lorrie like this, and, wondering what was the best thing to do with her, finally decided to let her alone, and let the beauty of the day and the influence of the service do their own work on her.

Unfortunately Miss Heywood, catching the girls up as they entered the gate, passed Lorrie, who was lagging behind, and with a hasty, "Keep up, there," went into the porch. This left Lorrie the only person not in church, and on a sudden impulse she turned back from the door and seated herself in the long grass out of sight.

From within the old ivy-covered church she

could hear the organ pealing forth, and the high
sweet treble notes of the choirboys. Tears sprang
to her eyes—thinking of Combe Langley Church
this morning, and Daddy taking the service, and
Mummie, with a white set face, kneeling there
asking God to make Timothy well again. Or
perhaps Tim was too ill to be left, and Mary
would be in her mother's place, with only Jackie
beside her, and Daddy would be praying more
earnestly than ever—and Tim would be lying
tossing on his little bed up in the nursery.

Why had God let this happen? she asked herself. Why hadn't He heard her prayers for help
during this term? Could anything be more unlike what she had prayed for than this state of
unrest in which she found herself? She wanted
so hard to do well and be a credit to them all at
home—but Prunella was like some evil spirit,
always there to goad her on to bad temper, which
led to bad work. Miss Heywood seemed to have
what June would call a " down " on her—and
now her darling Timothy was ill, and she was
miles away and unable to help.

When the girls came out and lined up into a
" crocodile ", Lorrie slipped into place beside
Judy and no one appeared to have noticed that
she had not been to the service with them. Judy,
of course, had missed her and said sadly: " I

wish you had come, Lorrie. I think it would have comforted you."

She remained in a defiant mood until Wednesday dawned with a high sky and golden sun. No lessons were held that morning, and by eleven o'clock the whole school was in the quad, lining up for the short walk through the fields to Fourteen Acre Woods. Honour was marshalling the girls into a crocodile. She said, hastily counting heads: "Who's missing in the Third?"

"Oh, Lorrie isn't here," June exclaimed, leaving her place and coming over to where the Third were standing. "What's happened to her?"

"She's gated," Prunella said in a sad tone. "It seems a dreadful shame, but she *is* so dreadfully stubborn and lazy. Nonnie gated her last week, I know, because Lorrie told me so herself."

"Oh, that's nonsense," Honour said cheerily. "No one is ever stopped from coming to the Head's birthday treat. Go and find her, Judy, and tell her I'm sure Miss Heywood forgot it was the picnic day."

Judy rushed away joyfully. Lorrie's miserable mood had thoroughly upset her, and she thought if she came to the picnic she would surely cheer up and be her gay, laughing self again. But, search through the school as she might, she could find no trace of Lorrie. She hunted through the form-rooms and dormitories, calling her name, but with no response.

Unhappily, at last, she joined the girls in the quad, who all shouted as she came down the steps: "Hurry up, you're keeping us all from starting."

"But she *must* be there," Honour said impatiently, as Judy told of her search.

"No *must* about it. She sneaked out without doing her work last Wednesday, and she didn't come to church on Sunday, so she's probably hopped off now, under the impression that we should all be too keen on getting to the woods to worry about her," Prunella said, with obvious satisfaction.

"Oh, shut up, you sour old Prune!" June said, digging her in the ribs with the handle of an old racket she was carrying. "Lorrie seems to have rooted herself most firmly in Nonny's bad books, and I think the poor kid's having a miserable time of it. What can we do, though, Honour? If you tell Miss Heywood she isn't here it'll mean a further gating, and a dreadful rumpus into the bargain."

"As Miss Heywood gated Lorrie, we had better leave it at that," Honour said sportingly. "We will all forget that I sent Judy to find her.

Maybe she really *is* inside somewhere, and is getting on with her work. You might try to remember that, Prunella," she said pointedly. " Come along, then, girls, we'll start."

Actually Lorrie was in the school! She watched the gay cavalcade march off up the hill, and her eyes were misted with tears. Never had she felt so utterly lonely and depressed. She had locked herself in one of the bathrooms, so that should Miss Heywood relent at the last moment, she would not be able to force her into going on the picnic. How could she enjoy herself, she thought, while Timothy lay ill, and while her own affairs were so unsatisfactory?

Some demon of restlessness, born of her un-usually depressed state of mind, urged her to go out. After all, why not? What possible harm could come of breaking bounds, even though Miss Heywood had forbidden it?

She glanced at the imposition Nonny had given her—a whole long précis and three verses of French translation! It was a dreadful punishment for so slight a fault as going down town last Wednesday.

The school seemed unutterably dead and quiet. Miss Heywood had joined the other mistresses, who had gone to the picnic-place in the Head's car. She had forgotten poor Lorrie and her troubles—" Very well, then," said Lorrie rebelliously, " I'll forget *her* and her rules!"

She had never been outside the gates in any direction except the town. Now she turned to the right and swung along in the fresh autumnal air, revelling in a sort of uncomfortable joy at her stolen freedom.

The road wound pleasantly along between the grey stone walls of the school for some distance, then there came a crossroads, and, thinking the sooner she left every vestige of Devenham behind the better she would like it, she crossed the road and went down the sandy lane opposite. Here again were high stone walls, with evil-looking pieces of broken glass on the top, and, every now and then, a notice nailed to the tall trunk of a tree, warning all and sundry that " Trespassers would be prosecuted ". Lorrie, to whom such a notice was always like a red rag to a bull, was musing upon the unpleasant type of owner the estate must have, when she heard a shrill cry coming from within the walls.

She darted nimbly across the road, and finding a spot where the bank rose higher, ran up it and succeeded in finding a foothole in the worn stone, and somewhat tortuously climbed to the top. The broken glass served as a good lever to pull herself up by; she threw one leg inelegantly over the top, and found herself astride the wall, with the branches of a chestnut within her reach, so that, should she wish to drop to the other side, help was ready at hand.

Across the beautifully kept parkland a little boy was running, and screaming as he ran. Just behind lumbered a man with a dog on a leash. They came towards where Lorrie from her leafy perch watched them, at the rate of knots, as she said afterwards.

" What's the idea?" she called indignantly, forgetting her own danger in her indignation. " I say, what's the idea of chasing that child?"

The man made indignant noises and checked his flight to look up at the tree from which it seemed the voice had come. The little boy had fallen on his knee, and lay only a few yards from the panting dog. He seemed unable to run any more, and was now crying in a most despairing manner.

" Where are you, you varmint?" the man called, still searching the boughs of the chestnut. " I'll set the hound on yer, you thieving wretch."

" Oh, will you," Lorrie said, launching herself on to the branch nearest and coming with it to the ground, in one rather frightening swing. She picked herself up and walked boldly out into the open.

She Plays Truant

"Now what is this all about?" she demanded angrily.

"Got yer," the man said, snatching at her shoulder as if she were about to run away. "I'll have the law on yer for this, my fine young lady. I'll get the police in to you and to this young rip here." He kicked out at the prostrate figure on the grass.

The little boy stumbled to his feet at the mention of the police, and would have started off on his flight again, but the dog snarled and snapped at his legs. The boy's face went a shade paler, and he seemed unable to move from sheer terror.

He was a good-looking little boy, but he was too thin and white, and his eyes were too big for his baby face. Lorrie saw his much-darned coat, and took in the significance of the bulging pockets of it!

"What has the child done?" she said, shaking herself free from the detaining hand of the keeper. "Stolen a couple of apples, I suppose? As you have ground enough here to grow millions of bushels, I shouldn't have thought the crime justified you scaring the wits out of the poor little chap."

"Who do you think you are, saying what I'm to do with the thieving varmint? From the school you looks to be, by yer frock. The master'll have something to say about you, young lady, climbing and a-scrambling over walls, and a-trespassing and using language to me, over the likes of a young ruffian like this one." He jerked the boy by the collar of his coat, and commenced shaking him until the child's head went from side to side.

Lorrie sprang at him and hit out. The man stepped back and eyed her vengefully, then he lumbered towards her as if he would shake her too. But Lorrie had sized him up, and realized why it was he had not caught the small boy before. He was a big, clumsy man, heavy and slow on his feet. She seized the little boy by the hand and ran off, skirting the wall and dodging in and out of the trees in an attempt to confuse her pursuer; and she might have succeeded, but that the boy's strength was already spent, and his terror of the dog, which the keeper had now unleashed and which was barking at their heels, made a drag on her. She gave it up, as, having come several hundred yards, she could still see no sign of the walls giving way to gates or open fields.

"Don't be afraid of the dog," she said at last, standing still and waiting for the keeper to catch them up. "Dogs are nearly always nicer than people. Come here, old boy," she said, holding out a friendly hand to the Airedale. The animal seemed to be afraid of the man, for he slunk to her side and, with big mournful eyes on his master, lay at her feet.

" Now what do you propose to do?" she asked.

" This," the man said, and caught her hands in a tight grasp, slipping the dog-lead round them. He then grasped the little boy by the back of the neck and proceeded to push him along. For a few steps Lorrie struggled, and then, as the keeper said he intended to take them to see " the master ", she gave in.

" This will mean the sack for you, you beastly bully," she said. " I'll see your master all right, and tell him the sort of person you are. Unless he is as foul as you are, you'll find yourself out of a job."

" Oh, so you thinks like that, do you? You don't know the master. He'll 'alf skin the hide off of both of you, a-sneaking his fruit and then be'aving like lunatics."

He walked on in silence for some distance, and Lorrie had time to realize her plight. Well, this probably meant the end of her career as a Devenham girl! The picnic party would return and find her accompanied by this dreadful old man, the master, and probably a policeman from Guildford! The story of her behaviour would be related, and the Head would pack her off there and then. A wire would be sent to the Rectory, she supposed, and with all the worry of Tim's illness, there would be this new trouble! In her imagination she saw Miss Forsythe, secretly elated, saying again and again that she didn't know *what* to make of the Rectory children —so undisciplined, so impossible!

They had come to some outhouses, and, to her horror, she saw that the keeper meant to shut them up in one of them! He opened the door of what looked like a disused stable, and forcing the whimpering little boy through, shoved Lorrie in after him. She started to protest, but her only answer was a slammed door and the sound of a key being turned in the lock!

CHAPTER VII

Prisoners

As her eyes became accustomed to the dim light, Lorrie saw that they were indeed in a stable. On one side was a feeding-trough, and to the beam in the wall had been attached a number of horse rings. The little boy, still whimpering softly to himself, had cast himself down on some rotting hay in one corner.

"Don't cry any more, old son," she said in much the same tone as she would have spoken to Timothy. "They can't really do anything to us, you know. That man was full of bluff. You wait until I see his master and explain. He'll get put in his place."

"I don't want no police a-coming after me, I don't," he snivelled.

"Police—nonsense," she said with more confidence than she felt. "You haven't done anything wrong, except steal some apples. How many did you get, by the way?"

"Only free," he said, taking them from his

pocket and eyeing them hungrily. "Can I eat 'em, please?"

She sat down beside him, although she had great qualms about the hay. She wondered what her father would expect her to say to the boy— ought she to tell him how wrong he had been to "scrump" the apples? Certainly he would advise her to give the child a chance of returning the stolen fruit. Not relishing the job of " preaching ", she said gently: " I don't think you really want to eat those apples, do you? You *did* steal them, after all."

" I want to eat somethink," the boy answered pathetically.

It struck Lorrie then that she knew nothing at all of the child's story. She said anxiously: " When did you have a meal last?"

"Do yer mean somethink to eat? Never 'ad a thing since yes'day dinner-time."

"Dinner-time? Do you mean to tell me you've had nothing for nearly twenty-four hours? Here, get on with this," she said, hastily pushing one of the stolen apples towards him. Surely Daddy wouldn't be " Rectorish " over a case like this? " Now tell me at once all about yourself—who are you, and what are you doing wandering about stealing apples?"

" I'm Johnny Radlet," he said through his

mouthful of apple. " 'Ere, miss, I don't want the police to git me fer eating this apple."

" Oh, stop worrying about the police. Where is your home?"

" Whitechapel," he said, then added: " I come with the Mission, I did, only I never wanted to go 'ome cos I likes this place. Crumbs, 'tain't 'alf lovely night-times, ain't it—all quiet and still. I wasn't 'alf scared, but all the same I liked it. I don't want to go 'ome no more," he ended, as if he had made the case quite clear.

" But what about your mother? She must be half crazy with worry."

" Ain't got no muvver. I lives with me auntie. She won't worry cos of me; she's got all her own to worry about, Susie and all of 'em. She told me I'd like it, and I do. I runned away when we was going through them woods. There was a bird singing fit to bust 'imself. I fort to meself, I couldn't 'alf do with a bit of this 'ere. So I dodged Miss Parsons—that's our Sunday School teacher—and I went running 'ard as I could. She can't run, you know. Funny, ladies can't run, can they? Must be 'orrible."

So he had escaped in Fourteen Acre Woods, where, at this moment, the Devenham girls were having a lovely picnic. It must be lunch-time— the sausages would be sizzling in the frying-pan

which balanced precariously on the log fire!
Hey Nonnie No would be cutting thick slices
of bread, while Miss Cranford of the Sixth would
be making a huge teapot of tea for the Seniors.
And here was Johnny Radlet, starving!

" Where did you sleep last night, then—in the
fields?"

" Yes, under one of them things made of
straw, what looks like an house," he said with
contentment. " It was ever so warm with some
straw on me, and I thought I 'eard a mouse
gnawing somethink close to me ear. Just like
Mickey Mouse would, you know. Then this
morning I waked up and I started to walk to
find somewhere where they'd give me work to do.
I ain't 'alf strong. 'Ere, feel me muscles."

He rolled up his sleeves and held out a skinny
little arm in her direction. She felt it obligingly;
it was hard because it was bone. She nodded
approvingly. " How old are you?" she asked.
He said he was nearly twelve! He was so small
and slight, she had thought he couldn't possibly
be more than seven.

" You can't get work to do at twelve," she
said seriously. " You'll have to make up your
mind to go home until you're fourteen at least.
Does your auntie beat you?" she asked.

He laughed at the idea. " No, of course she

don't. She's ever so nice to us. It wasn't nothing like that made me run away. It was all them lovely great trees, and them big fields full of lovely wet dirt what they'll put corn in next spring, Miss Parsons says. I never seen nothing like it before, though, of course, I've read about it. I never believed it, though I can believe anythink now, though, now I seen them trees."

" I wish I could help to keep you here, Johnny," Lorrie said, mopping at her eyes which had filled with tears. " But when you are bigger you can come back. Come down to Combe Langley and I'll make Mr. Lay at the Combe Farm give you a job."

" Would yer really? Pucker dinks?" he asked anxiously.

She said she most certainly would, but at the sight of his pathetically thin face and sunken eyes, she wondered what possible job on a farm he could do.

There was a sound from outside, a clinking of pails and the sluice of water. Lorrie sprang up and peered through a crack in the door. She could see a large fat woman emptying a pail and swilling down the yard with a hard broom. She called: " I say, how long are we to be kept in here? I demand to see your master."

There was a gasp of dismay, and Lorrie was

amused to see the woman cautiously approaching the locked door. " For mercy's sake, who are you?" she whispered through the crack.

" Your keeper has shut us both up here. I am a Devenham girl, and I have a boy of twelve with me. Can you get us out of here, please. This little boy has had no food since lunch-time yesterday."

" Bless my soul," she said, and threw up her hands in amazement. She waddled away towards the house, muttering something about, " Tom Salter do take too much on 'imself, he surely does."

" She'll get us out of here," Lorrie said confidently. She wondered if even now she might get back to school before she was missed. She had no previous experience to go by, but she thought probably she mightn't be missed by the picnic party, except her own friends, and they would think she was still at school doing her impot. At the school, Matron would imagine she was with the rest, and so between the two she might, if she got back before the others, escape undetected. But what on earth was she going to do about Johnny?

Hers was not the type of nature which can dismiss anything difficult as " none of my business "—the mere fact that circumstances had thrown her and Johnny together made it her duty to help him all she could. Had she been nearer home, she would not have hesitated to take him to the Rectory, waited to see him with a big bowl of milk and some food, and left him to the kindly mercy of Mummie and Daddy. But alas, the Rectory was miles away and she was penniless!

There was the sound of several pairs of feet clattering over the cobbled yard. The key was put in the lock and the door thrown open. The brilliant midday sun flooded in through the open door, and the two " trespassers " stood blinking in the strong light.

" Come you out of there," said the keeper's voice, and he strode forward and hustled Johnny before him, but the fat woman interposed.

" Here, you give over that sort of behaviour," she said indignantly. " And I'll have you know, Tom Salter, as I won't have you a-locking people in my shed where I keeps me odd brooms and things. Fine thing if I'd a-gone in there and not knowed—would have fritted the life out of me. Come on now, miss, bring the little chap in the kitchen, even if he is the criminal what Salter says he is. He must have a bite and a sup in his innards before he sees master."

" Criminal," laughed a young girl in a neat cap and apron. " Tom's been to the pictures down

Guildford way, seemingly, and the gangsters have gone to his head. Come on, sonny; not a day more than ten, he isn't, is he, miss?"

"He says he's twelve," Lorrie said, smiling at the toss of the head the girl gave to the keeper as she passed.

"Then he isn't your little brother? Oh no, I can see now. You're from the big school, seemingly."

They entered a large flagged kitchen, clean and neat, with hams hanging from the rafters and enormous pots bubbling on the old-fashioned grate. Lorrie saw Johnny's head go up, like a dog sniffing the scent, at the smell which wafted from the stove. The fat woman, whom Lorrie judged to be the cook, lifted Johnny on to a chair as if he had been a baby of three, and quickly filled a basin with soup. She cut a huge hunch from a loaf, then stood back and seemed lost in admiration at the picture she had created.

Certainly it was good to see the boy eat and drink. He never stopped until the bowl was empty. Then his first words were: "Thank you very much, mum, that went down fine. Could you stop your husband a-getting the police? 'cos I ain't done nothing, only pinched them apples, and I wouldn't have done that only I was so clemmed."

Prisoners

" He ain't no husband of mine, thank heaven,"
she said piously and with deep gratitude. " You
haven't got to worry about no police, my son—
it's the master you've got to think about."

" So the keeper said," Lorrie put in, noticing
how Johnny's eyes dilated with fear. " I can hardly
imagine a gentleman being angry with a small
boy for stealing three apples. I will see him now,
if I may. I must get back to school as soon as
possible."

" You can't see him before two o'clock, miss,
'cos he mustn't be disturbed before lunch and
not till half an hour afterwards. He's not like
most gentlemen, the master—he's got a most
wicked temper, really he 'as, and trespassing's
one of the things he goes nearly mad about. I
don't want to frighten you, miss, but he *is* a
hard man, though he has his softer moments. I
never knew old Salter to actually catch anybody
before, but I've heard the master say what he'd
do with 'em if he ever *did* catch anybody trespassing on his land, and it doesn't sound nice, I
can tell you."

" There is no need for you to look so frightened,
Johnny," Lorrie said, seeing how terrified the
child had become. " I shan't let this old man
hurt you, you trust me. Does your master live
alone?"

"Yes, miss. He ain't got neither kith nor kin, as I knows of. I been with him this twelve year, and nobody ain't never come here to stay, except two old gentlemen from London, friends of Mr. Crighton—that's the master," she added.

The servants stood looking at the two tres-passers as if they were of some unknown species. It was obvious from their faces that they were sorry for them, but it was also obvious to Lorrie that they were enjoying the situation. The house must be rather a lonely one, she thought, so big and rambling, and holding only this dreadful old man who lived the life of a hermit, it seemed.

As the novelty of their presence wore off, the servants began to get on with their work. The pretty maid went along the passageway carrying a tray and obviously going to lay the luncheon-table, while the cook busied herself by the stove, "dishing-up". Tom Salter stood just outside the back door, as if to guard it in case his captives tried to escape. Not much hope of that, Lorrie thought, remembering that long dismal drive with its overgrown bushes and gloomy trees; long before she and Johnny had reached the gates they would be overtaken and dragged back by the unpleasant Salter.

She edged to the door and looked along the dark passageway. Johnny, looking all the better for his meal, came and stood beside her. "Do you think we could do a guy for it?" he inquired anxiously.

"No, I don't," she whispered back. "The road is too far from the house; they'd only catch us again. Don't say anything, or attract the cook's attention. I'm going to creep down this passage and find this old man and have it out, now, at once. I can't wait here half the day until it pleases him to see us. Don't be frightened, Johnny, I'll get round him somehow."

"You ain't done nothink, it's me," he said, with a frightened gulp. "I ain't going to let you go alone, miss, it's my funeral, not yours."

"That's the spirit, Johnny," she said, looking down at his thin little figure. He had pluck, if he had nothing else, she thought. "I'm not going to let you come, though," she added. "I'll do better alone. Don't let them know I've gone."

She crept on tiptoe through the open door and along the thick-carpeted corridor. She could feel her heart beating in her throat, and the sound of it seemed to fill the narrow passage. It was absurd, she told herself, to be so frightened of any old man on earth. She was quite innocent of anything except trespass, and that, she remembered with a grin, she had been guilty of at home scores of times. The servants seemed to go in fear of their lives of this old "master"—but no man on earth, she told herself, could make her really afraid.

A baize sound-proof door confronted her; she pushed it open and came upon a square hall, light and airy, with windows thrown wide at one end on to a lawn. Out there, under the trees, she saw an elderly man pacing backwards and forwards, his head down and his hands clasped behind his back. She studied him for a moment before she went forward through the french doors into the garden.

At the sound of her approach he looked up and started. She was not surprised at his look of surprise because, of course, he was not expecting her; but his sudden whiteness and his absolute amazement at her arrival she found hard to understand. Was he so much alone that the sight of an ordinary schoolgirl could make him change colour like that, and totter towards his chair?

"Who are you?" he said in a whisper, almost as if he were afraid. "Who are you, child? What is your name?"

"I know what the mystery is," Lorrie thought, with a start of horror; "he's mad!"

"My name is Lorraine Grey," she said in a

tone as muted as his own. " I came to you because your keeper has been so perfectly beastly
to a little boy who was scrumping some apples.
But, you see . . ."

" Just one moment, please," the old man said,
raising a thin white hand to silence her. " Am
I to understand that you have forced your
way into my house to protest against my own
keeper?"

" Yes, that's it exactly," Lorrie said. He was
not mad, that was certain now. He seemed to be
recovering from his amazement, too, and in its
place she thought she had raised the smouldering
fire of his anger which the servants had dreaded
so much. Her own temper was not improved by
the fact that she was hungry, and that while she
stood here her hopes of getting back to Devenham unseen were rapidly dwindling. If this old
man were going to lose his temper, he would find
that hers would be a match for him.

" And where in this story of impudence and
trespass do *you* come in, may I ask?"

" I heard Johnny screaming in terror, and I
climbed the wall and saw the hateful Salter person
chasing the poor little boy—with a dog, too,"
she added, getting more and more angry as she
thought of it. " Salter managed to catch us both—
we were running away together, you see—and he

had the impertinence to lock us up in a stable. We were let out about half an hour ago, and I was told I had to wait to see you until after you had had your lunch, but that is out of the question, as I must get back to school."

"How dare you trespass on my property?" he thundered, rising from his chair and standing over her. "Do you think I'm going to have all the rabble of Hampshire stealing my apples and breaking down my trees and doing untold damage, and then be held to account by a mere slip of a schoolgirl?"

"I can't help being a mere slip," snapped Lorrie furiously. "As for damage, I'd be the first to stop damage being done to trees, but the child didn't *do* any damage. He was hungry; he'd had nothing to eat since yesterday lunch-time, and he saw some apples hanging on a tree. What do you think you'd have done?"

"Don't be impertinent."

"I don't mean to be impertinent," she countered. "But perhaps you've never been hungry; perhaps you've never longed for the country as Johnny does. Perhaps you've never lived in a London slum, and never believed such lovely things as trees in a forest really existed—and then had just one day in the country granted to you, and felt you could not go back. All that has happened to Johnny since yesterday, and instead of your keeper taking him in and giving him food, and listening to his story—he chases him with a dog, kicks him, and threatens him with the police."

"That's what Salter is paid to do."

"Then more shame to you. Yes, you can do what you like with me, I don't care. I'll be expelled from Devenham anyway, I expect, but I'll tell you what I think while I'm here. Do you remember the Prodigal Son? Well, I know Johnny isn't your son, except that we're all one family, really—do you remember The Good Samaritan too? Well, what have you to say about it? Or aren't you a Christian at all?"

"This is too much," the old man said. "First you force your way in to see me, although you have heard I must not be disturbed; then you preach to me, and accuse me of not being a Christian. How *dare* you?"

"It's you who is in the wrong, and you know it—I can see by your face you know it. I won't have that poor kid's nerve broken more than it already is—I *won't* have it." She knew that she was near tears—that was the way her temper always served her, first a flare up, and then tears of sheer anger. But added to this was the remembrance of Johnny's frightened face, and his brave attempt to shoulder his own troubles. This old man should *not* stand over him and bully him, as he was standing over her now!

"Do you know what he told me?" she continued in a quiet voice. "He told me he slept under the stars last night, and listened to the quietness. 'Crumbs, it wasn't 'alf quiet,' he said, and it was as if he were in a church, he sounded so awe-inspired. You can't frighten him any more with stories of the police, and all the rest of it. You can't, I won't allow it."

The old man strode into the house, and she saw him press a bell in the hall. When the pretty maid came through the baize door, her eyes all agog with excitement, he said curtly: "Send the boy in here to me."

He remained in the hall. Lorrie watched until Johnny, looking whiter and more scared than ever, was pushed into the hall by the maid and left standing there alone; then she walked back and stood beside him. The old man eyed them both without speaking. At last the strain was too much for him, and Johnny burst out, "Don't send for the police, guv'ner, please don't. I never stole nothing before, honest I never did."

"He isn't going to send for the police," Lorrie said calmly, though her knees were knocking together and her hands were cold as ice.

Prisoners

" What is your name, and where do you come from?"

Johnny repeated what he had already told Lorrie. The pathetic little story of the Sunday School outing came out, and Miss Parsons saying that corn was to be planted in the now fallow ground. Johnny, without meaning to, painted a picture of himself standing in the woods, looking up at the autumn leaves—red, gold, orange—seeing for the first time in his life the whole wide glory of the countryside, and thinking of the mean streets of home, and thinking, too, " I can't go back, let me stay here." " So I dodged Miss Parsons," he finished simply, " and 'ere I am."

As she watched the old man's face she saw it soften, and a smile flickered over his thin-lipped mouth. She could not have said afterwards what it was that so suddenly robbed her of all fear for this elderly man, and made her know, beyond any shadow of doubt, that her battle with him was over. She was almost as much surprised as he was to find herself taking him by the hand and saying in an almost motherly way: " Now, come on, don't please be cross any more. He is a poor little boy who needs our help. One day perhaps you'll need help too."

" Perhaps I need it as much as he does now,"

he said in a gruff voice; then in his normal stern voice he snapped: "Have you both had some food?"

"No, I haven't, and what's more, I daren't stop to have any," Lorrie said, feeling suddenly awfully light-hearted and gay. "I'm playing truant to-day, and if I don't get back I'll probably be expelled."

"I'll ring up the school and say you are here," was the amazing answer. "You can't go all that way back without food—I can't let you, or you'll be telling me I'm not a Christian!"

"Oh, I can't let you do that," she said, as he moved towards the telephone. "I'm not supposed to be away from school at all."

"Another hour won't make much difference, and I'll send you back in the car. Come along, now, we'll have lunch immediately. You must remember that violent young women do not break into my house every day of the week—I have a lot to say to you."

" 'Ere, guv'ner, what about me?"

"Oh, you, Johnny? Well, you go along to Mrs. Harris in the kitchen and tell her you'd like some plum-duff, and that I'll settle your fate after I've had my lunch." He rang the bell and told the maid there would be one extra for luncheon. The girl's face was a study of incredulity—

she went through the baize door backwards, her mouth open in surprise.

In the dark, sombre-looking dining-room, Lorrie found herself put at the extreme end of a long table which would have comfortably seated at least twenty people. The prospect of shouting to her host down the whole length of the table struck her as being funny. She said: "Do you think I could move up, nearer to you? I can only just see you from here! If I lived in this house I'd have all my meals in that nice square hall—this room, if you'll pardon me for saying so, gives me the 'dodderam-shacks'!"

The old man laughed, and his entire face changed. He looked younger, now that he no longer looked so stern and forbidding.

"I think you are right, Lorraine," he said. "Next time you honour me, I'll see that your orders are carried out. Tell me something about yourself—your people must be quite wealthy to send you to Devenham. It's a very expensive school, I believe."

"Oh yes, I think it is, but I'm a charity child," she told him quite cheerily.

"I should like the whole story from the beginning to the end."

"You shall have it," she said.

CHAPTER VIII

The Queer Old Man

Lorrie, whose starved senses were free at last to talk to someone who knew nothing of her own battles at school, plunged into a long account of home. She painted a picture of the lovely, rambling old Rectory with its crowd of children, and its charming, gracious mistress, and its tender-hearted master. She quite frankly talked of the poverty they all knew so well; but she made a joke of how she always had to have Mary's "left-overs", and how when they did go shopping, she once had said as Mary tried a frock on: " I don't think the colour will suit me, 'cos I shan't get it until it's faded!"

The old man seemed to have a passion for details, and made her describe the house, the long wide windows in the drawing-room, with " mother's " patch of delphiniums just outside, shining blue-white and silver in the moonlight. He seemed best to like that picture of them sitting in the twilight together, with the garden fading from rose-hued sunset to grey-blue twilight, and so to silvery moonshine! Lorrie saw it all as she told him——saw her mother's lovely chestnut hair, piled and shadowy against the shabby old rose-coloured cushions; heard again her soft laughter and her sweet, small voice singing to them the songs she and Mary had loved when they were quite little.

So entranced was she with her own word-pictures, that it was with a guilty start that she heard the deep chimes of a grandfather clock striking three.

" Oh, golly!" she exclaimed, jumping up as if she had been shot. " I *must* go. I'm sorry I've talked so much; it's one of my worst failings."

" I wouldn't have let you if I hadn't liked to hear you," he said, opening the door for her. " I will ring for Saunders to take you back; it'll only take a few minutes in the car. I shall have to send Johnny back to his aunt, you know; he is too young to leave school yet."

" Oh, what a pig I am—I'd quite forgotten Johnny. Oh, but couldn't you tell him he could come down here sometimes? The cook seemed to quite like him. Promise to have him for a week or two next summer—that's what my father would do—it'd break the blow for him knowing he could look forward to the country next year. I'll save up and help with his keep," she volunteered.

"I'll see," he promised. Johnny came from the kitchen quarters as soon as he knew Lorrie was off. He looked at her expectantly: "Ain't I never going to see you no more, miss?" he asked.

"Yes, you are," she said, taking the law into her own hands. "Maybe next summer, Johnny, you'll come down here to stay, and I'll come over every Wednesday afternoon and play with you. And if it so happens that you can't come here, you shall come to Combe Langley, and stay with us there."

"Oh, I wouldn't 'alf like that," he said, with eyes shining.

"And when will you come and see me again, my child?"

She looked up into the stern old face, and saw that he really did want her to come. "Strange," she reflected, "most grown-ups are only too pleased not to be bothered with me."

"I'm not really allowed to come—this is out of bounds for us—but I might manage to slip away one half-day."

"I am a lonely old man," he said, rather bitterly. "I have liked having you to-day. Come next week, my dear, if you can."

The Queer Old Man

An ancient Rolls Royce stood at the door, with an equally ancient chauffeur at the wheel. It was obvious that the man had been a groom at one time, and that he still regarded the car as an unpleasant invention. He wrapped an enormous fur rug round Lorrie's knees, and drove at about five miles an hour down the depressing-looking drive. Looking back, Lorrie saw the old man standing, watching the car out of sight, and she thought what a dreadfully pathetic picture he made. As they went through the great iron gates, she turned and saw on the stone pillars at the side, the one word—" Basseton ".

Where on earth had she heard the word before? Cudgel her brains as she would, she could not remember, yet she knew that the word was vaguely familiar.

At the beginning of the stone wall that surrounds Devenham, she told the chauffeur to let her get out. It was no part of her plan to arrive at the school gates in style!

She entered by the lower gate, which led by devious paths to the girls' entrance of the building. So far so good. Not a soul was in sight, and she ran nimbly up the stairs and along to the dormitory. Here she changed her outdoor shoes, which still retained some of the mud from the stable, and put on her indoor pair. She went quickly to the common-room and proceeded to write her précis. The day had been full of adventure, she thought, but it was not ended yet!

The girls returned, tired but happy, at five o'clock. A specially lavish tea was laid for them, and Lorrie joined them at it. The first person to greet her was Judy, who said in great disgust: "Where the dickens did you disappear to this morning? Honour sent me back for you, and I hunted the school and couldn't find you."

"I was in the bathroom over the porch. I watched you all go. I'm sorry, Judy. I've been in a beastly mood for days now, and I deliberately watched you, and I heard you calling me too, but I wouldn't budge. I'm not a very nice person when I've got a bad mood on me."

"I do wish you had come, though. It was a lovely picnic. Nonnie No asked where you were—asked me, of all people—and I was going to say you were in the common-room doing your impot, but I suddenly thought, suppose she sends someone back for her! I *was* in a dither, so finally I had to tell a lie. I tried to put her off by saying I didn't know where you were—which was the truth—but then she said, 'Is she still at the school?' and I said yes you were! As it happens, then, it wasn't a lie, and you were

The Queer Old Man

still here? Anyway, she didn't seem satisfied, and she said that of course she hadn't meant to gate you on the Head's birthday and to keep you from the picnic, and told me to run back and get you."

"Oh, Judy, what a beastly position I put you in. Well, what was the end of it? You came back and found the bird had flown, I suppose?"

"Yes. I went back and found Nonnie No, and said you had a headache. It was awful, Lorrie, because just as I was starting back to get you, I met the Prune, and she said, 'Oh don't *you* trouble to get Lorrie, I'll go,' and then she added: 'If she isn't in the school and the Head finds out she has spent the day on her own after being gated, she'll be expelled for certain.' Gosh, that girl does hate you."

"Hateful beast that she is," Lorrie said venomously.

"So I said there was no question of you not being at school, but she hung about, and I honestly believe she went back after I'd been, and looked for you herself. I wish to goodness you wouldn't go prowling about alone; you know it means trouble if you're found out, which you are sure to be, sooner or later."

As they went along to the c.r. June and Sally joined them, and they both asked Lorrie why on earth she hadn't come along. It appeared that Miss Heywood had asked all of them what had happened to her, and so had turned the attention of the whole school upon her.

The more she thought it over, the more selfish her own conduct appeared to her. She had forced Judy into a difficult situation, from which she had had to tell lies to escape, unless she told the truth, which might mean expulsion for her friend! And yet, mused Lorrie, if she *hadn't* played truant to-day, where would poor little Johnny Radlet be now? From the vicious speech of Salter, she thought the little boy might still be in the stable, forgotten, or worse, remembered only to be punished. It was amazing how goodness sometimes came from a wrong action, though she knew her father wouldn't agree with her theory.

But whether the end justified the means she went to bed doubting, for after supper Honour sought her out, when she was playing a game of chess with Judy, and said Miss Heywood wished to see her in her study immediately.

"Look out for squalls when Nonnie adds 'immediately'. It nearly always means that she can't wait to be unpleasant," June said sympathetically. "There has been something fishy about your behaviour to-day. Lorrie, now

The Queer Old Man

I come to think—to mix my metaphor—Nonnie is on the scent of it!"

"It means expulsion if the Head hears that you have been out of school all day on your own business," Prunella put in. It struck Lorrie suddenly as being odd that the Prune should be in the c.r. just then, looking on in that infuriatingly superior way of hers. Most of the Fourth were down in the gym playing Badminton. June was there because she was playing off a chess match that she had now won against Lorna Bray—but why was Prunella standing there?

Lorrie didn't answer the remark, but she noticed that Judy had gone rather pale. "I shan't mention you, if I have to tell the whole story of to-day," she said.

"I don't relish the idea of Miss Heywood finding me out in a deliberate lie," Judy said. "I've never told a direct falsehood before, and I feel beastly uncomfortable about this one."

"Lot of fuss about nothing," muttered Lorrie, as she mournfully made her way to Miss Heywood's study. But things seldom turn out as we think they will. Miss Heywood greeted Lorrie warmly.

"My dear child," she said, looking at her pupil's white face. "I can't tell you how sorry I am that you should have stayed in to-day, instead of coming to the picnic with us. I quite forgot that it was the Head's birthday, or I should never have gated you on this, of all days. When I discovered that you were not with us I was really deeply troubled. I sent Judy Grenville back to find you, but apparently you were hidden away with a headache, and couldn't bear to come. Do please understand that I should not for one moment have allowed you to miss the picnic for any other reason than illness."

It was a great relief to realize that she didn't know; on the other hand, it made Lorrie feel rather small to have her mistress sympathizing and apologizing, when she knew that in fact she had been herself entirely at fault. If it weren't for the fact that Judy would have to be given away, Lorrie would have confessed, there and then, that she had not stayed in all day with a headache. But with Judy to shelter, what could she do? She stood miserably before Miss Heywood, feeling utterly contemptible.

" I know I have been rather hard on you lately, Lorrie," Nonnie went on, heaping coals of fire on poor Lorrie's head; " but I simply *have* to make you study so that when you come back next term you will be in the Fourth. It is dreadful that a bright, intelligent girl like you should be down with the Juniors in the Third.

I don't want to make your first term a nightmare, goodness knows, but I do want you to be in the Fourth next term with girls of your own age."

"Oh yes, I know that," Lorrie stammered. "I want to be in the Fourth too. I hate being down with the Third, and I *have* tried this term."

Miss Heywood came towards her, and placed a friendly hand on her shoulder. "I know you have, my dear," she said in a curiously softened tone. "If you were not worth helping, I should not bother so much about you. Now run along to bed, and remember that when I gate you, I don't mean to stop you coming to picnics or anything special. And, by the way, I think you should be specially nice to Judy Grenville, because I believe she would do a lot for you."

This last remark seemed to Lorrie to carry a double meaning. Was it possible, she wondered, that Nonnie No had seen through Judy's falsehood, and had overlooked it because it was done for a friend? As usual, the Prune was the first person to encounter Lorrie as she walked back to the common-room.

"Well, did she find out that you were not here to-day, and that your friend was forced to tell absolute lies to get you off expulsion?"

"Mind your own beastly business and keep

out of mine," Lorrie said furiously. " If a lie to save a friend were the only sort *you* told, there would be something to say for you, but yours are all the sneaking, vicious variety. Lies you deal in, and a little cheating and gossip—the worst sort of human vices there are!" She had culled all that from one of the Rector's sermons, she realized as soon as she had said it.

Prunella's face was scarlet with rage. " Oh, you just wait. I might have let you off all the other scores I have against you, but not now— not after *that*. Do you think my aunt would pay for you to come here if she knew that you were sneaking out for whole days together, and telling lies and getting your friends to lie for you? Do you think she would allow you to come to Devenham where *I* am if she knew your lessons would disgrace a kid of six, and your place in form so low that even Miss Heywood gates you —and has you in for private ' jaws ' to her study . . . do you think——?"

" Yes, I *do* think!" Lorrie said, suddenly hitting out. " I think it's time I taught you a lesson once and for all."

So that once again, the scene that met Honour's eyes was of Lorrie and the Prune, fighting like cats on a wall. She separated them, and, telling them to come to her study the next day, sent each in her own direction, and walked away absolutely disgusted with them both!

But strangely enough, with the thought of yet another black mark against her name, Lorrie was not nearly so downcast as she had been the last few nights. She had a feeling that Tim was better, and that things at the Rectory were altogether brighter. For the first time for several nights, she said her prayers before she hopped into bed. She went to sleep, to dream of the stern old gentleman whose face could soften so completely as to change his whole appearance. " I'll go and see him, the first chance I get," she thought, when she awoke the next morning.

But before the morning session was over, the Prune had had her revenge! She had mentioned, quite casually, of course, and with *such* a surprised look when Miss Heywood was annoyed, that *she* too had been back for Lorrie, and had found that, as had so often happened lately, Lorraine Grey was out.

It was during the only lesson Miss Heywood gave to the Fourth, and this, as the Prune had seen, was her only chance of getting her blow in. Miss Heywood took the Fourth for Biology twice a week. The Prune considered this her best subject, and she actually was the best in form, so that Hey Nonnie No often praised her and stood talking to her about her paper after the rest of the form had gone. This she unhappily did the morning after Lorraine's adventure.

"Such a pity Lorraine was out all day yesterday, Miss Heywood," the Prune said casually, collecting up her books and preparing to depart. "It was such a lovely picnic, wasn't it? I'm sorry my aunt's protégée missed it; the Rectory crowd get so little pleasure."

Miss Heywood did not take up the "aunt's protégée" lead, but said sorrowfully: "Yes, I am sorry the poor child thought I had gated her on the Head's birthday. But as she had such a bad headache, I suppose it would not have done for her to come, in any case."

"Bad headache?" the Prune said wonderingly. "Then why on earth did the silly girl go out alone all day, roving the countryside. So bad for her if she was not well!"

Miss Heywood looked intently at her, and the Prune had the grace to blush—sometimes Nonnie No showed more insight into one's motives than was comfortable.

"What makes you say Lorraine was roving about the countryside?"

"Well, she was—she often does. She went off alone instead of coming to church last Sunday.

The Queer Old Man

Of course one can't say anything to her, she gets so furious."

"That is enough, Prunella, you may go!" Miss Heywood's tone was condemnatory. Well enough she knew that the Prune was out to make trouble for Lorrie, and for a split second the mistress wondered if she could, just this once, overlook the offence. But cutting church without special leave was an offence which the Head herself always dealt with—and as for being absent from Devenham without leave and alone for a whole day—it was a crime hitherto unknown!

CHAPTER IX

A Network of Troubles

Miss Heywood waited until after morning school before she said to Lorrie as the girls filed out: " I want you a moment, Lorraine."

Lorrie, remembering how perfectly charming she had been the day before, turned back into the form-room quite cheerfully. She was the more surprised at the grave look Miss Heywood gave her.

" Where were you yesterday?"

Lorrie felt the colour leave her cheeks—how on earth *could* Miss Heywood have got to know of her absence from Devenham?

" I was here at school, Miss Heywood, until long after you had all gone to the woods, then I went for a walk alone."

" In spite of the fact that I had gated you?"

" Yes, I'm afraid so." She wondered whether to say how miserable she had been lately about Tim's illness, but decided not to try to get out of trouble by working on the mistress's sympathy.

" And where were you, when you should have been in church last Sunday?"

Oh gosh, she knew *everything*! Playing truant

A Network of Troubles

yesterday had been risky, but cutting church last Sunday, when only Judy seemed to miss her, had seemed fairly safe. Who on earth besides Judy could have noticed her absence?

"I stayed just outside the porch. I could hear the organ and the hymns," she added, as if in extenuation.

"Did you know that cutting church without leave is an offence the Head herself deals with?"

"No, I didn't know anything about it. I was fed-up with everything, and something prompted me, just as we were going in, to turn aside, and so I did."

"Well, I'm afraid whatever prompted you was working for your downfall. I could have dealt with you for going out after I had gated you, but Miss Graham will have to know of your repeated absences, and I am afraid she will take a very serious view of them. I shall put you in my report this evening. I am sorry, Lorraine. You may go."

Puzzle as she would as to who could have given her away about church, Lorrie could not think of an answer. She might have jumped to a correct answer of her problem if she had noticed the Prune last Sunday, but she hadn't. Prunella was at the head of the church crocodile and Lorrie was at the tail, and so it did not occur to her that the Prune would be on the look-out to make trouble, and so would slew round in her pew to observe Lorrie, and so find, to her intense satisfaction, that her pew was unoccupied.

By the midday post came a letter from the Rectory, and in it Mummie put:

"MY DARLING,

"Tim is better, thank God. He has really been most awfully ill—worse really than we let you know, because we didn't wish you to be miserable and worried about him. Dr. Green says he is now definitely out of danger. The only problem Daddy and I now have to settle is how to send Tim away to the south of France to recuperate. Dr. Green says the sunshine is absolutely necessary—but he doesn't tell us how to make the money to send Tim—it means that either Nannie or I must go with him, and just at the moment I cannot see how to make it possible. However, my darling, never fear, God never 'lets us down', so all will be well. Daddy and I are both so glad to hear that you are happy and settled—and we are so proud of our 'really truly schoolgirl', as Tim calls you.

"All our love to you, darling,

"MUMMIE."

A Network of Troubles

And so they were proud of her! And how would they feel when they heard that she had " cut " church on Sunday, and played truant on Wednesday, and was in Miss Heywood's report to the Head for both offences! Why, oh why had she been such a fool as to go madly on her own way, just because the Prune had got on her nerves— the Prune and Tim's illness!

He must have had pneumonia really, then, she mused, picturing Tim tossing on a burning-hot pillow, and a steam-kettle going, and all the other horrors of a sick-room. She wondered if it would be possible to appeal to Miss Forsythe to devote the money she was now spending on her to Tim instead. Even one term's school fees would be sufficient to send Tim and Mummie to France for a month, she thought—and how much more good the cash would do, saving Tim's life, perhaps! But then she remembered that by the time Miss Forsythe received her letter asking her to transfer her help, the Prune would have reported that Lorrie was in disgrace —if not actually expelled!

The rest of the day was an absolute nightmare to her. By tea-time she had decided to take Judy into her confidence, for the weight of her trouble seemed too much to bear.

" But how on earth did Nonnie find out about

last Sunday?" Judy said, looking worried. "I must say, you know, Lorrie, that you have behaved stupidly. Where *did* you get to yesterday, or don't you want to tell me?"

"No reason for not telling you," Lorrie said mournfully, and she told her story. Judy was excited about it and pleasantly impressed.

"If you told the Head that story she would let you off for sheer pluck," she said enthusiastically. "I bet there isn't another girl in this school, except perhaps June Martin, who would have dared to climb that wall and face that angry keeper. You're a giddy heroine, Lorrie, and I'm proud of you."

It was a great comfort to hear Judy's words. It really hadn't occurred to Lorrie to think of her actions of yesterday as anything but the normal thing for a girl to do. But to Judy, to whom a barking dog, an infuriated keeper, and an elderly gentleman with an awful temper would have been too frightening for words, Lorrie's actions seemed almost on a parallel with those of Florence Nightingale herself!

"It's sweet of you to try to cheer me up by saying that," Lorrie said gratefully. "But the fact remains that I didn't *know* I was going to rescue Johnny when I left the school—I merely thought I'd let Nonnie and her gating go hang;

A Network of Troubles

I'd amuse myself in my own way, for once. I realize now that Tim's illness had worried me more than I cared to admit even to myself, and instead of confiding in you and getting you to help me with your sympathy, I preferred to keep all my feelings bottled up inside myself! Ah well! the Head can't eat me—she can expel me, of course, and then I'll go home and Daddy will be ' Rectorish ', and Mummie will be dreadfully disappointed, but——"

She ended her long speech in tears, because, try as she would to put a cheerful complexion on the matter, it *was* sickening to be returned from school just when the people at home were proud of one—and just when their attention was engrossed on bigger and more important things.

" I don't mind betting that somewhere at the bottom of this mess the Prune has had her finger in the pie," said Judy, getting involved in her own references. " I feel convinced that she came back yesterday and found you gone. She knew, in that case, that I had told Nonnie No a lie when I said you were resting because you had a headache, and she must have decided to let Nonnie know in some way, so that she would ask you the direct question—and I suppose she knew that you wouldn't tell a lie as easily as I did."

" This conversation makes the case look blacker than ever," Lorrie exclaimed. " I hadn't realized before that if Nonnie knows that I was out all yesterday, she must also know that you told her a fib! Oh dear, I wish to goodness I hadn't involved you in this."

" It doesn't matter," Judy said determinedly. " Look here, Lorrie, let's go down into the c.r. and wait there until the Head sends for you. It's no good putting Gay Campbell's back up, and she's got a sports meeting on. We'll go and join in."

Down in the common-room the girls were all squatting on the tables, chairs or floor, listening to Gay. A few Fourth-formers were present, and Lorrie was hailed by Sally and June as soon as they saw her.

" Good for you, Lorrie Grey," Sally sang out.

" Why, what have I done?"

" Well, it appears that you *can* use your legs enough to play hockey, if you *can't* use your brains enough to get into your proper form," the Prune said.

" I should have thought you'd have had enough of having your ears good and soundly boxed, to have said a thing like that," Lorrie said grimly, and went towards Prunella, who, as usual, had bagged the window-seat.

A Network of Troubles

"Here, keep her off." The Prune dodged behind Kitty Dean of the Fourth. "I can't compete with the Rectory Brawn and No Brain Combination."

"Oh, shut up!" snapped Gay. "I'm conducting a meeting, Prunella Forsythe, and so if the Fourth can't behave decently, it can jolly well clear out—the Third have the majority and it knows how to use it. Lorrie, I'm putting you in the First Eleven as half-back to see how you shape. If you don't come up to scratch, Lilian Brooks will have to have your place—you've won by a short head, really, because there isn't a great deal between you and Lilian, but of the two you are slightly quicker. If you get impots on half-days, though, you'll go, because I must have the whole team and the reserves on the field by 2.30. Now about the badminton fours——"

"Lorrie," whispered Honour, coming in quietly, "the Head wants you."

Outside the door she said kindly: "I suppose you had forgotten that I wanted to see you, too, for fighting so disgustingly with Prunella?"

"Oh heavens, yes, I *had* forgotten," said poor Lorrie dismally. "The truth is, I'm in such a lot of separate hot waters that I haven't time to dive into each of them!"

" Well, as far as I am concerned, I'll forget I saw you pulling handfuls of Prunella's hair out! What *have* you been up to, my dear kid, to get into Miss Heywood's report?"

" You know how they read out about people being ' missing from their homes ' on the radio —well, I was missing from the school, and some clever person managed to inform Miss Heywood. It's no good, Honour. I've come to the conclusion that I'm a mistake at Devenham— the old Glory-hole at the Rectory is the place for me."

" Nonsense," Honour said briskly. " You are just the type we want at Devenham, but you'll have to learn that rules are made to be kept—that seems to be something you've never really grasped!"

The Head's " Come in " sounded like a death-knell to Lorrie, whose heart was beating up in her throat somewhere, and whose legs were doing their usual flapping! The study was lovely, she thought, trying to keep her attention off the subject of her crimes. A huge fire burnt in the old-fashioned grate, and the warmth of it had drawn the perfume from the bowl of chrysanthemums on the desk, so that the air was delightfully scented. The Head was seated in an easy-chair by the fire, and, to Lorrie's surprise, she motioned to her to sit in the opposite one. This didn't *seem* like the wigging she had been fearing. "Now, Lorraine, I should like a full explanation of your conduct since last Wednesday."

"I did half my imposition on Wednesday, and then went down to the Yellow Lantern with June and Gay Campbell. Miss Heywood found out, and gated me for this Wednesday. Well, everyone went out to the picnic and I was alone, so I thought I'd go for a walk. I went and didn't get back until about four o'clock."

"What about church on Sunday? I see in Miss Heywood's report that you did not come in to the service, but sat outside until we came out."

"Yes, I did."

"Have you no excuse to offer? Don't be foolish enough to think that silence is best in things like this. I feel sure that three offences so quickly happening one on top of the other would never have been committed by a new girl unless she were worried or miserable. If you had been here more than half a term, I should have to punish you severely, but I think, as you have only just come to school, I must be lenient with you—at the same time, I must ask you to give me some explanation."

Gradually the story of Tim's illness came out —and the blow the Head had dealt to her pride in putting her down in the Third with girls younger than herself—and her longing to possess that blue cubicle, and to be put up with June and Sally! She deliberately avoided any mention of Prunella's hatred and persistent beastliness, because anything at all in the nature of " sneaking " was foreign to her.

" But, my dear child, I *told* you that your time in the Third would be short if you worked hard, and Miss Heywood tells me you *have* worked well, and that she feels sure your terminal report will justify me in putting you into the Fourth. Are you such a baby, Lorraine, that you couldn't accept your low position for a short time, until you could earn your reward?"

" I suppose I must be," Lorrie confessed shamefacedly.

" Well, please don't be in future. Now tell me, where did you go yesterday?"

Very briefly, just in case the Head should think that she was making a heroine of herself (this wouldn't have occurred to her if it had not been for Judy), she related how she had climbed the wall of the estate and had been locked away with Johnny—and had finally been persuaded to stay to lunch with the " old gentleman ".

To her surprise, since the Head seemed to be in such a forbearing mood, her story seemed to worry Miss Graham. She said sharply: "Was the name of this house 'Basseton'—and was the old man's name Crighton?"

"The house was certainly 'Basseton', though I didn't know that until I was being driven away. I don't know what the owner's name was, he didn't say."

"You must understand this, once and for all: I absolutely forbid you to ever go near 'Basseton' or to see Mr. Crighton again. Do you quite understand that, Lorraine?"

"Yes, Miss Graham—but why——?"

"I'm not in the habit of explaining my reasons, Lorraine, but do please understand that Basseton is out of bounds for you, and if I ever hear of your going there again, the consequences will be extremely serious. Now run along, my child. I feel that now your mind is at rest about your brother, you will stop being disobedient and babyish, so I shall not punish you at all; but please, as you value being at Devenham, do not let me hear of your breaking bounds again."

Lorraine went out more puzzled than she had ever been. That there was some mysterious reason for the Head's anger at her visit to Basseton she knew as well as if Miss Graham herself had told her. She rushed to the common-room and found Judy standing silent while the rest of the girls were round the piano, singing. As she went in she noticed that the Prune, who was standing with Sally, looked up interestedly, and seeing Lorraine still looking cheerful, appeared disappointed!

"Well, was it as dreadful as you thought?" Judy whispered, leading Lorrie towards the window away from the singers.

"No, it wasn't. Both the Head and Nonnie No are great sports—I don't know what they'd be if one had been here a term or two, but for a new girl they make all sorts of allowances. But, Judy, there is a mystery about Basseton—and I'd love to solve it, but if I ever go near the place again I think it'll mean expulsion."

"Well, it's out of bounds, that's enough in any case. But what's the mystery?"

Lorrie told her of the way the Head's face had changed as soon as the name of Basseton was mentioned—she described the worried look that the Head had worn as she talked of Mr. Crighton. "It wasn't just a case of my having broken bounds, but of my having been inside Basseton that infuriated and worried her," Lorrie ended.

"Don't say any more now," Judy cautioned. "The Prune is looking *so* interested in your expression. If she can do you a bad turn, she will."

A Network of Troubles

"I believe she already *has* done her worst. I'm sure it was she who put Nonnie No on my track. Nonnie was sweet to me last night, but by this morning she had heard something more — this Basseton business — and was after me again. There isn't another soul in Devenham who would take a malicious pleasure in letting her know that I was out yesterday."

"Anyway, you seem to have weathered your storm well. I do hope to goodness you'll not do another single thing to start trouble. It just isn't worth it, Lorrie. It isn't worth a wigging from the Head to fly at the Prune and beat her up as you do; and it certainly isn't worth the risk of being expelled to break bounds. So I do trust you'll put the thought of Basseton out of your mind, and not go snooping about trying to solve the mystery of the wretched place."

"I quite agree with all you say, oh learned one," Lorrie said, bowing with mock homage before her friend. "Actually, I feel as if the air is cleared. Tim is better, and the Head knows of my escapades, and now I can start all over again. I *do* wish I knew what the mystery of Basseton *is*, though."

CHAPTER X

Christmas Shopping

After the storms of the last few days, it seemed to Lorrie as if she had reached calm at last. She realized that her extra tuition was given her for her own good, and most sensibly made up her mind to profit by her mistress's zeal.

On half-days she worked hard at hockey. She knew that the difference between her play and that of several other Third-formers was very little in her favour, and she decided that whatever happened, besides getting a good percentage in the terminal exams, she would keep her position in the First Eleven too.

The Prune still did her best to make trouble, and also to be as irritating as possible, but now that she was on a different understanding with Miss Heywood, and knew that, stern as the mistress was, she was still just (a beast, but a just beast, as Judy quoted), she was not easily influenced by cutting remarks made by Fourth-formers against members of the Third.

Christmas Shopping

Meanwhile, Sally and June, on the few occasions when the girls all met, still made a point of being particularly nice to Lorrie. They talked as if it were a foregone conclusion that Lorrie should be with them in the Fourth for the Spring term, and they still spoke of that dear little blue cubicle, which was still unoccupied, as "Lorrie's cube"

The weather turned from mellow autumn to cold winter in one night, it seemed to Lorrie. On Wednesdays now, she was on the practice field from the first moment she was allowed until the last, and the cold weather setting in seemed to have banished the rain, and the girls were able to play for four consecutive half-days, which, said Gay joyfully, was jolly nearly a record.

If Lorrie thought at all of her half promise to visit old Mr. Crighton again, the remembrance of the Head's warning made her banish even her regrets. After all, she mused, if Basseton were so definitely out of bounds the old man could find out that it was for himself, and then he would understand why she had not visited him. The more she thought over Basseton and its mystery, the more she wished the Rectory crowd, including John, lived nearer Devenham, so that in holiday-time she could help to unravel the mystery that surrounded it. As it was, the Head had made it impossible for her to ever find out more about that lonely old man and that great gloomy mansion. She wondered, too, about Johnny—was he sent back that same day, or did the old man keep him for a day or two until he had got in communication with his auntie? Was he to be allowed to come back to Basseton next summer, as she had suggested—or had the old man said good-bye to him, and thought "good riddance"? Somehow, remembering how Mr. Crighton's face had softened into a smile as Johnny told his story, Lorrie couldn't see him being hard on the little boy.

Judy puzzled about Basseton too, but with the exams coming on in a few days now, and with Christmas presents to make in one's spare time, and with the thought that, as a reserve, she might, in the event of one of the eleven getting a sprained ankle or something, be cal'ed upon to play for the First, she had no time to try to solve the mystery.

The Wednesday before the exams dawned hard and cold. Miss Penn, the sports mistress, said the ground was too hard for play. Gay, of the Third, and Sally, as sports captain of the Fourth, both protested violently that time was too short to spare time for mere hardness of ground. Miss Penn smiled at their enthusiasm, mentioned broken legs and fractured thighs, and said she was afraid that, with ten degrees of frost, the ground made play quite impossible.

"I don't know that I'm as upset as I ought to be," Lorrie said in the common-room after dinner. "I want to get most of my presents for my people down here, because at home we've only a few poky little shops, and we often buy the same things and solemnly give them to each other!"

"Oh, so do we," Gay said with a grin. "Mother gives Daddy a pound note to buy something with, and he gives her a pound note —and I give my brother half a crown, and he, stingy blighter, usually gives me a bob and says he'll make it up later when he has more money. As he never has a bean, I never get it!"

"It must be too horrible to be as hard up as that," Prunella said loftily. "What money have you to spend, Lorrie?"

"Well, as we're all only allowed the same shilling a week, I should have thought you knew."

"Oh, but I wondered if my aunt gave you your pocket-money as well, or if she left it to your people to do *that* for you, in which case I suppose you wouldn't have even a bob?"

"Strangely enough, my people *do* give me my pocket-money, and I *do* get a bob," Lorrie said savagely.

"Why do you let her draw you like that?" June said, coming over to her. "She knows perfectly well that you have the same as the rest of us, and that your people pay it. She says it to make you furious—and she succeeds! As for you, Prune," she said, swinging round and facing Prunella, "I can't think what's happened to you since Lorrie came. You were never one of the most delightful people on earth, but at least you weren't as foul as you've been this term. Sally and I are fed to the teeth with your absurd snobbery and beastliness, and you'd better cut it out unless you want to find yourself in Coventry."

It was a long and angry speech for June, who, as a rule, was a person of few words, and was much too happy-go-lucky to mix herself up in other people's quarrels.

Prunella went quite white. For her chosen "crush" to speak to her like that! It was ridiculous, she realized, to have such a "crush" on June Martin, but she had had it now for years, and until this dismal term she had persuaded herself that June liked her fairly well. Now, because of Lorraine Grey, it seemed June hated her.

"Come on, let's clear out of this atmosphere of fury," Gay said cheerily. "As we *can't* play, we might as well do as Lorrie suggests and go down town and do some shopping. I'm the proud possessor of five bob, and out of that I have to buy at least five presents!"

"Thank goodness for Woolworth's," Lorrie said, forgetting her anger at the thought of spending the precious four shillings she had saved by not buying a single thing for the last five weeks. She had managed to eke out her spending-money by putting tuppence-halfpenny in the collection on the last four Sundays, and by looking the other way when she went past the tuck-shop! Four shillings was not too bad, she thought, and she only meant to buy two presents out of it—one at say half a crown for Mummie and a one-and-sixpenny one for Timothy.

"As you think so horribly of me," Prunella said bitterly to June, "I suppose you won't let me come shopping with you, though I have for the last three Christmases."

"Oh, sink your wretched grievances and get your coat and hat and *come*," June said impatiently. "Who else wants to come? The invitation to accompany me—which is a *great* honour, of course—is open to all!"

It was no use, in the face of what June had just said, saying that if the Prune went, she certainly was not going, thought Lorrie, though really she would much rather have stayed behind than go with Prunella.

"June has put you in a rather awkward position," Judy said sympathetically as they went down to the cloakroom. "But as half the school seem to be coming along, it shouldn't be difficult to give the Prune the slip. I want to go to Harrington's to buy some crash. Coming with me?"

Lorrie said she would, especially as she also had thought of patronizing Harrington's for Mummie's present. She mused, as the whole party of girls clattered merrily along the hard frosty road, that one's "crushes" were difficult to understand. For some reason she couldn't fathom, she was more pleased by a friendly overture from June than she was by the warm friendship which Judy offered her. She realized that she was getting the worst of the bargain, for June was surrounded by friends—in fact, the whole Fourth seemed keen on her—whereas Judy was prepared to be a "special" friend, who would give all her attention to her alone.

"Do you think my father would rather have a tie than a gramophone record?" Sally was saying thoughtfully, kicking a stone along as she went in what Miss Heywood would have termed a "singularly unladylike manner".

Christmas Shopping

" Not if it's anything like the scarf you bought him," giggled Kitty. " Do you remember, June, it was red with yellow spots, and touches of pea-green here and there! What the Surrealist people would probably diagnose as a channel-crossing during a gale!"

" Don't be so disgusting," Sally said in an outraged voice. " It was jolly becoming. We had snow after Christmas, and Daddy tied it round the neck of a huge snow man he made."

" Best thing he could do with it too," June said witheringly. " I think men are *awful* to choose things for. I've given my father three different coloured pens, and he has always broken them by the next Christmas, so I just give him another. I rather thought of giving my brother Keith a pair of garters—goodness knows his socks are always round his ankles! It would be rather a joke to give him a lady's pair—you know the things, they sell them in Woolworth's; they are pink satin ribbon with flowers on the side!"

Lorrie had almost made up her mind to try to get a few nice but inexpensive hankies for her mother, and a clockwork Mickey Mouse for Tim, who had a passion on Mickey. She confided her plans to Judy, who said she was going to get half a yard of crash and some very stiff cardboard, and make a *Radio Times* cover out of it, embroidering the front in lazy-daisy stitch. Her aunt, she opined rather sadly, would be fairly sure to find fault with it, whatever it was, but there was no doubt about it being useful.

Once in the town, the girls separated into various groups. The Prune stuck as closely as she could to June, in spite of their former battle of words. Judy and Lorrie went into Harrington's, and Judy got just the quality crash that she wanted. For a long time Lorrie pored over the handkerchief box, first thinking the embroidered ones were nicest, then perhaps the plain. Judy gave it as her opinion that the white linen with the pale-blue embroidery were by far the nicest, and at last Lorrie succumbed to them though they left her with hardly any money for poor Tim's present!

Once away from the glamour of that hankie-box, she began to wish she had not been quite so extravagant, for Woolworth's had no clock-work Mickeys, and the only shop that had was charging too much for them. To her surprise, the Prune, seeing her standing alone while Judy chose her coloured cottons, came to her side and said in a friendly manner: " I saw you looking at those clockwork toys. Did you want to get one?"

Christmas Shopping

"Well, yes, I did rather—I wanted one for Timothy. I've spent nearly all my money, though, so it's out of the question."

"I can lend you a shilling, if that would help;" then she added, seeing that Lorrie was about to refuse: "You can pay me back when Nonnie gives you your pocket-money on Saturday."

So she could, of course, and this was probably the last time she'd get to town before the school broke up, and then she would go straight down to Combe Langley, and there were no lovely clockwork Mickeys there for Tim. Her pride bade her refuse absolutely, but she asked herself, was it not false pride when Timothy, not she, would be the one to suffer if she turned down the Prune's offer. "It's awfully generous of you. Are you sure you don't want to spend it yourself? Haven't you things to buy?"

"I shall do all my shopping in London," the Prune said superiorly. "You are quite welcome to the bob if you like—it'll only lie in my purse if you don't use it, and you can certainly pay me back on Saturday if you like."

"Well, then, I think I will," Lorrie said gratefully, and added: "Perhaps you'd like to come and help me choose it?"

"Oh no, thanks," Prunella said, her voice

quite changed once she had handed over the money. "Children's toys don't interest me much, I'm afraid." She walked off quite quickly and joined June and Sally at the perfumery counter.

Lorrie wondered what had suddenly changed her and then changed her back again! Perhaps just for a moment, she thought, the spirit of Christmas had entered into her—the sight of the very premature Father Christmas in his red cloak and his enormous white whiskers, handing out toys from his sack to a delighted crowd of children—or the Christmas tree growing out of its tub, ablaze with fairy lights and tinsel— perhaps these things had softened the Prune's heart for a moment, as the sight of Little Tim had softened Scrooge's heart in *A Christmas Carol*. Well, whatever it was, it was jolly nice of her to lend the shilling, and it made all the difference to the whole afternoon.

The Mickeys were intriguing! They walked along, swinging their arms—or they turned somersaults! The shopman set three of them working at once, and the rest of the girls crowded round to watch them.

Lorrie bought one that turned somersaults, and, with her two precious packages, went to seek Judy at the cotton counter. She was not there, but the assistant said: " She has gone across to Brown's. We hadn't any needles quite suitable for the crash, and she has gone to get some."

Off went Lorrie, found Judy, and, thinking they would catch the rest up if they walked quickly along the road, started off. They were both rather hungry by this time, and when they came to the Yellow Lantern, looked with longing at the cakes in the window, and sniffed like Bisto children at the smell of hot crumpets that issued from the door. To their amazement, there at a table were June, Sally, Kitty and the Prune. June hailed them delightedly.

" We can't come in," said Lorrie in a stage whisper. " We've spent all our dough!"

" Really, Lorraine, what an expression!"

Lorrie followed up her *faux pas* by falling down the step and into the shop. For the voice was the voice of the Head herself.

" Sorry, Miss Graham, I didn't know you were there," she stammered.

" No, so I gathered! Well, since you are here, and I *am* here, come in and have tea. Yes, you too, Judy."

The girls sat down opposite Sally and June, and the Head and Miss Penn continued their interrupted conversation at the near-by table.

It was lovely coming in from the cold to this

warm little café with its big fire, its hot crumpets and tea! And all the more enjoyable, thought Lorrie, because it was so unexpected.

"Wasn't it luck, my dears," whispered June across the table. "I just poked my nose in to see if Honour and Co. were here, and the Head saw me and invited us all in. We were watching like cats at a mouse-hole for you two to come by! More butter, please, Rose," she said to their favourite waitress. "And some more milk if there is some going."

When the first pangs of their hunger had been overcome, the girls all undid their parcels and displayed their purchases. True to form, Sally had bought a large silk handkerchief for her father—white, with a scarlet border. As she said complacently, if he didn't like it, it would come in most beautifully for a peasant scarf for her, next summer!

June had bought a pair of gloves for her mother, and had spent her cash, so Keith, she opined, would have nothing but good wishes!

Raising her voice above the tone the others had been using, Prunella said chattily: "I lent Lorrie some money to buy something she wanted —she also had spent more than she meant to."

Lorrie felt the colour flooding her cheeks, as

she realized that the Prune's voice had carried
and the Head was looking at her inquiringly.

"Don't talk so loudly, you half-wit," muttered
June. "Lorrie, you're a fool, always flouting
rules and regs."

"I didn't know there was a rule about borrowing," Lorrie said miserably. "I didn't ask
Prunella to lend me the wretched shilling; she
pressed me to take it."

"That won't stop the Head being furious
with you if she finds out. Oh Lord, why can't
we have a bit of peace this term. You and the
Prune seem constantly in trouble of some sort."

"I think it's pretty despicable of Prunella
to press Lorrie to borrow money, and then to
try to get her into a row about it," Judy said
indignantly.

"I didn't try to get her into a row," Prunella
protested. "I had forgotten the Head was
there."

"In any case, why mention it at all? And it's
a jolly funny thing you spoke more distinctly
than any of us."

"Oh, for the love of Mike, stop wrangling.
You and your quarrels, Lorrie. They seem to
spoil almost every outing we have together."
June spoke quite bitterly.

Tea finished in an unfriendly silence, and

Lorrie was glad when the Head rose to go, and they could go too.

Out in the road was the Head's car, but blocking the way was the ancient Rolls Royce in which Lorrie had once gone rolling back to Devenham. She wondered now if, should Mr. Crighton appear and speak to her, the Head would come forward and tell him that both he and his house were out of bounds to Devenham girls. But, to her amazement, when he did appear, he greeted the Head most affably!

"Oh, here's Mr. Crighton," Prunella said excitedly.

"Who is he?" asked Judy.

"Don't you know him? My dear, he is most fearfully wealthy—and he's one of the Governors too. He has a lovely house here, called Basse-ton. I don't want to sound snobbish, but I believe he is a descendant of the Dukes of ' Bas-seton' in some way—anyway, he's a frightfully good family, but such a hermit. He hardly ever comes to speech days or anything public."

"Then why, since he seems so entirely all he should be, should the Head have had a blue fit because I saw him?" Lorrie asked herself. When she discussed it afterwards with Judy, she agreed that the plot not only thickened—it was nearly solid!

CHAPTER XI

Miracles Happen

The great day of the Exams had come! Miss Nesbit, head of the Kindergarten, was " vigilating ", and Miss Heywood had descended to take the Kindergarten exams. A deathly silence, which could be felt, descended upon the Third; then, as the papers were read, a sigh here of horror, a gasp there of relief, as girls either realized that the questions were " too utterly awful " or " really *not* too bad ".

" Everything rests on the next three days," Lorrie thought, hardly daring to look at her paper. " Miss Forsythe will undoubtedly decide whether to keep me on at Devenham, or to let me stay at home, by what marks I get in my report." She looked down at her English paper —perhaps it wasn't *so* bad after all.

They had taken *King Lear*, and the first question was: " Show how, in Act 4, the various episodes of the play are working themselves out, and how each bears on the main plot."

She worked hard at that, giving, she thought— re-reading her page and a half of close writing—

a very fair answer to an involved and difficult question. It was the sort of thing she knew she did well, as often at home they had read plays together, before acting them to the village, and Daddy was so marvellous at pointing out how a play took shape and form, and how a clever author drew his characters and incidents neatly together before the climax of his play.

The other two questions she selected from the list of six were: " Give the context to and explain the force of the following expressions— ' Oh, no, I know the riddle; I will go ': and ' The wheel is come full circle; I am here '."

During " break " the girls got together and discussed the paper. Little Fay Carter, who was well known to be in Nonnie's bad books, said she had selected the question to supply meaning to, "I am a man—more sinned against than sinning ", and had put in a long account of how she herself *knew* the feeling! " If Nonnie No can't make the cap fit, she's not as wary as I think she is," she said with a grin.

Judy said she hadn't liked the questions very much, because although she knew the work, her memory was rotten when it came to remembering long and involved speeches, so she hadn't been able to do much with the context questions. She was hoping better things from the précis.

which they were pretty sure to get that afternoon.

Sure enough, they were asked to write a précis of a long letter written by William Pitt in the first person, of course, but to be written by them in the third person! Lorrie, looking with wide eyes at such passages as, " I shall not lay myself under any restraint, nor very solicitously copy his diction or his mien, however matured by age, or modelled by experience ", echoed the groans of the rest of the form, but worked steadily through the whole long, involved, difficult letter, and, at the end, reviewed her short précis of it with satisfaction. On the whole, she thought more cheerfully, the day had gone better than she had expected.

Once up in the common-room, pandemonium broke out afresh. The girls rushed at the Fourth-formers with yells of " What *did* you get?" " Ours was *hopeless*!" " That wretched William Pitt, and his ghastly letter—I'll bet his friends didn't read his letters, if they were all like that one." " What exactly *did* he mean when he said he wouldn't attempt to ' palliate ' nor deny the charge? I said, ' He wrote that he would not be a pall, nor would he deny '."

There was a burst of laughter from the other girls, and Sally said the idea of the great Pitt using a word like " pall " was rich.

From what the others were saying, Lorrie felt

she hadn't done badly, and at Judy's suggestion, they crept up to the Fourth-form dormitory and gazed fondly at the little blue cubicles, which they hoped next term would be theirs.

Next day there was a letter from Mary, and after a gruelling morning at maths, Lorrie took it thankfully away to the shrubbery, and there in seclusion read:

"Darling Lorrie,

"A miracle has happened! Yes, a really truly miracle, like you read of in the Bible. I know we always say we believe in them, but in our hearts I don't believe we expect them to happen in these modern days—anyway, I know I don't, and Daddy, in spite of his faith, is *amazed* —and suspicious!

"Did Mummie tell you that Tim ought to go to the south of France for the winter? Well, it was quite impossible, of course, and the most we could scratch together, pooling our doctor's fees and all the extra cash from the holiday fund and everything (including your moneybox too), was enough for Honney to take Tim to Bournemouth for three months! But—last Friday came an anonymous letter — not even registered — with a London postmark, and in it was a note— typewritten—and it said, 'For your own family', and there were ten fivers too! I honestly thought Mummie would go crazy, she laughed and cried at the same time, but Daddy was awfully worried about it, and if it hadn't been for the note, would have put it straight into the Medical Missions At Home box. Anyway, it means that Tim is to be sent, with Honney (Mummie says she can't leave all the rest of us), to a lovely village, near Grasse, for six months, when, old Dr. Green says, he'll be ' fighting fit again '.

" We've puzzled our brains ever since Friday, but there really is *nobody* on earth who could do it—Daddy says he knows hundreds who *would*, but not one who *could*. Anyway, Tim is off on Monday, and I am to take lessons with Daddy until Honney comes back—and Jackie is going over to the Hawthorne's to study with their horrible governess!

" I've never written such a long letter before in my life! But it's all been so exciting. I ought to have written the moment it happened, but I've been helping to get Tim's clothes ready—seems to me that my job in life is seeing you all off, and waving you good-bye!"

Poor Mary, reflected Lorrie, she hadn't meant that last little bit to sound as bitter as it did! But the miracle! Straightway, without a doubt in her heart, she crossed to the school chapel, went quietly in and slipped to her knees. She had doubted that prayer helped, and still she remembered how awful she had felt those few days when she had omitted her short evening prayers, and had shut her heart to the help they would have given her. Now, when something really dreadful had threatened the Rectory crowd, God had sent, in some mysterious way, the very material help which was needed to save Tim. Her eyes filled with gratitude; God must have *such* a lot to think about, and yet he had listened to the pleading of her own little family. Never again, she vowed, would she forget the *personal* in His love for them.

The news of the miracle worked another miracle! The exams passed like a dream. Lorrie forgot all the really good work she had put in this term, and was amazed when she found that she was translating difficult French, answering geographical questions knowledgeably, and doing really remarkably well at history.

Judy was pleased with herself too, and the two of them went happily off after the last examination paper, and drank each other's healths in ginger-beer at the tuck shop.

This last few days, Lorrie had seen nothing beyond a few glimpses in the common-room of the Prune. In her present forgiving state of mind, she was prepared to think the best of Prunella, and to put a kinder interpretation on her behaviour in the Yellow Lantern than a few weeks before she would have done.

The Exams finished on Tuesday, and the Inter-Form match was on Wednesday, followed by a breaking-up supper, and on Friday they all went off! It was a sombre thought that they would all spread out, into villages, towns and cities all over England, in a few more days—while here they lived in this one big building, a little community safe against the world.

The match, which the Head was going down to watch, began at 2.30. Lorrie, inwardly seething with excitement, tried to keep cool outwardly by taking a book of poems in her hand, and, muffled up to the eyebrows with scarves over her scanty hockey kit, strode up and down the quad. She was conning the lovely words of Stevenson's romance: " I will make you brooches, and toys for your delight," she said aloud.

" Hi, miss!" The voice came from the top of the wall—just as the last time these two had spoken, *her* voice had come from a wall-top.

It was Tom Salter. He was wagging his head, just above the wall, for all the world like a wax-work, Lorrie thought.

" Do you want me?"

" Yes, miss. The master said if I seen you I was to say why bean't you come nigh him, like you said you would?"

" I'm not allowed to," she said, in what she hoped was a low enough voice not to carry across the quad. " Basseton is out of bounds, and I shall get expelled if I go there."

" Not you! Why, the master is one of the Governors of Devenham. Girls comes to the house in the summer, to garden parties and I don't know what all. The master—he don't see 'em, of course—shuts himself up in his study those days. But you could come all right, miss, if you wanted to, and master be right bad this time too."

" Bad? Do you mean he is ill?"

" Aye, that I do. Doctor coming all the way from London three times in a week—turrible ill he is. It's his heart is bad. He've asked if you've showed up many a time this last week."

She couldn't have said why she suddenly felt so dreadfully upset about an old man's illness. After all, he was nothing to her, she told herself, and she had known of elderly people being frightfully ill before, yet never had this sickening feeling about them. Suddenly, as if compelled by some unseen force, she heard herself say:

Miracles Happen

"I'll be over at Basseton as soon as the match is over. Go back and tell your master—I'll be there by five."

It meant expulsion—the Head's most severe censure—disgrace. Why, oh why had she laid herself open to all these things for the sake of that bad-tempered old man? But even as she blamed herself and called herself the world's fool, she knew in her heart that she could not have refused to go. The old man's loneliness had made a deep impression on her that day she had lunched with him. She recalled now how he had stood, bareheaded in the afternoon sunlight, watching her drive off in the old car. Everything about him spoke of loneliness, and to Lorrie, who all her life had lived surrounded by a lovable family, loneliness was the most dreadful sadness one could suffer.

Why, she wondered, did he old man ask for her? What possible comfort could a girl of her age be to the stern "master" of that vault of a house? "But perhaps," she thought, "he feels the same strange friendliness for me that I instantly felt for him—as if, in some queer way, we 'belonged'."

Of one thing she was certain. She would be expelled if she were found out—so—she *wouldn't* be found out! The more she thought of it, the more she was certain that in going to the call of a lonely and ill old gentleman she was doing no wrong. It was the sort of thing Daddy would approve of—he couldn't be so " Rectorish " as to maintain that because of some utterly futile regulation she should not do what she could to bring comfort to someone in need.

No, it was *right* to break a rule sometimes— but it would certainly be to the good if she were not found out!

" Where on earth *have* you been ?" Judy cried, suddenly coming round the corner and cannoning into her. " I've been searching everywhere. Come on quickly, we're due to start in five minutes."

On the field the mistresses and the rest of the school were grouped under the trees—almost as if their leafless branches could protect them from the biting east wind. Gay had the team round her, and was giving them last-minute instructions about passing. Lorrie, she said, was the worst offender at hanging on to the ball, and passing when it was too late. Lorrie promised to remember her warning. The whistle blew and the match began.

Gay, herself, was the heroine of the day! She played as if inspired. The Fourth played an attacking game, and Gay realized the only hope her side had was to defend their goal and wait until some crucial moment arrived, and then attack.

By half-time the score stood equal at three goals a side. The Fourth changed their tactics as they changed sides—playing a wary game, and when they got the lead by one goal, they tried to keep it by playing for safety. It was within two minutes of close of play that Lorrie, rushing up the field with the ball, saw Gay on her left; she was tackled by Sally, but managed to dribble the ball through and make a pass to Gay. By this time the Fourth were shouting their heads off, and the Third were too excited and keyed up to do more than clench their fists. Gay, running like a hare and dodging like one possessed, shot a magnificent goal. A second later the whistle blew!

It was one of the best Inter-Form matches for years, the girls agreed, and the result was certainly a popular one. Lorrie was surrounded on all sides by girls telling her that she passed—for once in her life—just at the right moment. Her enthusiasm almost made her forget her promise to go up to Basseton, but a glimpse of the Head, smiling encouragingly in her direction, reminded her and she sped off to the dormitory to change.

She had already formed her plan carefully, and

was rather annoyed at her own craftiness in being able to plan an escape from the school which she told herself was " foolproof ".

She meant to go to Nonnie No immediately after she had changed, and ask if she might start her personal packing when the Fourth started theirs, immediately after tea. She was sure Nonnie would give her permission as she was a great believer in " getting things done in time ". Having already got permission to be absent from the common-room, she would then appear at the tea-table, whisper to Honour, who was " taking tea ", that she had Miss Heywood's permission to pack (she needn't say that was what she *was* going to do, she comforted her outraged conscience), and so slip away from the table early. She would go to the dormitory with a pile of school books, open her tuck-box, and leave the floor strewn with obvious signs of packing—then if Nonnie looked in, she would conclude that Lorrie was down in the common-room getting more things to pack, and if she went into the common-room would conclude that she was in the gym or some other part of the school, collecting her goods from borrowers. Looked at from every angle, she could see no " snag ".

She carried out her plan without a hitch. Several girls heard her make the arrangement to pack her personal things, before Matron had time to do it for her, and they did not think this at all queer, as the Fourth always did their own, and any Third-former could if she gained permission. The others were still at tea when Lorrie, feeling like a " spy " in a drama, crept past the school and gained the road.

She had time, while she hurried along the silent country road, to wonder why on earth she was taking all this trouble—and risking so much too—for the sake of an old man whose temper, to say the least of it, was touchy. She knew that her father, being asked to attend a sick-bed, had never been known to refuse, or to put off going. But it was his *job*, while hers was to do as she was told, and not to disobey the rules of Devenham. But the old man seemed so helpless, in spite of his great house, his servants and his bad temper. He had roused an almost motherly feeling in Lorrie—he was like a naughty child who is " sorry now ". But, she laughed to herself, such a thing was absurd; in reality he was a man of means who chose to shut himself away in his house and surround himself with notices saying " Trespassers will be prosecuted ".

Now that she knew the way, it took her only ten minutes' quick walking to reach the desolate drive with its gloomy-looking shrubs and its leafless branches meeting overhead. The house itself looked as if it had fallen asleep—its eyes closed with dark blinds.

She pulled at the bell and heard its muffled peal go through the house and re-echo back again, as if the summons had gone to rouse the occupants, but had returned from its quest unsuccessful. She waited a few moments and was about to ring again when she heard footsteps and the great door swung back.

" Oh, so you managed to get here, miss." It was the pretty parlourmaid. She looked young and alive and fresh, and Lorrie's doubts and gloomy forebodings fled from her.

" I told Salter I'd come," she said, entering the hall. " Is your master very ill?"

" Well, I've seen him just as bad before, but he seems more miserable this time, if you get my meaning. We tried to get him to have the nurse he had last time, but he wouldn't, so Cook and me have had all the extra," she ended, obviously sorry for herself.

It occurred to Lorrie that there could be little work for the pretty maid to do, as there was only one elderly man to wait upon, and four indoor servants to do it. She hurried up the dark stair-case after the girl, walked along the passage, and together they stood outside a door, waiting to

be allowed to enter. At last there was a feeble
" Come in," and in they went.

" It's the young lady from the school, sir."

" Oh, Lorrie. Come in, my child."

Lorrie went into the bedroom, and was immediately struck by the change in the old man. In
bed, he looked only half the size he had seemed
to be when they had met before. His face was
pale, and there was a tired look in his eyes which
took the sternness out of his face entirely. He
reminded her of someone, she couldn't think
whom—or perhaps it was a picture she had
seen; anyway, she knew that she was glad she
had come—whatever the consequences. She ran
forward impulsively, and took his thin hand in
her own warm grasp and said: " I ought not to
have come, but I'm awfully glad I did. Have
you been dreadfully ill?"

" No, nothing more than usual, but this time
I seem to have noticed the loneliness more, and
my books seem to have lost their power to comfort me. Miss Graham would have let you come
if I had sent the car for you, wouldn't she?"
He asked this question so searchingly that somehow Lorrie *knew* that, for some obscure reason,
he feared that she would not have been allowed
to visit him, car or no car.

" It's awfully queer," she said confidingly;

" but although I saw you talking to the head, and she seemed so pleased to see you, she was *livid* when she knew I'd been here. She has put you and the house out of bounds for me, and she says she'll have to send me home altogether if I come here again——that was before I came, of course."

" I was afraid of that," the old man murmured to himself; then he said: " And so you've braved her wrath and the threat of expulsion, and all the rest of it, to come to see a sick old man who needed you?"

" I don't see how you need me, exactly, but I know how it is to be ill and want people always buzzing in and out. I had chickenpox once, and I used to howl blue-murder because Mary and Jackie and Tim weren't allowed to come. I had Mummie and Daddy, though, so I wasn't left alone for long. I'd have brought you a jelly and a William pear if I'd been able to——it's funny how I always long for jelly and pears when I'm ill——do you?"

" No, I haven't noticed it, but now I come to think of it, I do remember another small girl who always wanted jelly when she was sick. Lorrie, what would you like for Christmas? That was one of the things I wanted to see you about."

Miracles Happen

"That's awfully decent of you," she said thoughtfully. "As a matter of fact, though, as I'll have to explain all about you to the family in any case, and probably have Daddy being frightfully 'Rectorish' at me for breaking rules, I think you'd better not give me one. I'll feel more comfortable too, because I've spent all I've got at the moment on Mummie and Tim, and I'll only just have enough for the others when I collect the rest of my pocket-money at home. I'll send you a letter, though, of course," she added.

"What do girls of your age like for presents nowadays? I remember at thirteen they used to still play with dolls, and they liked books like *Little Women*, and gloves were beginning to be popular with them, and autograph books."

"Well, gloves are only an awful responsibility, I think," Lorrie said, speaking from past experience. "They get lost, at least one of them does, and then your family all read long lectures to you, and you have to carry one glove to church, and a fine fool you look! *Little Women* is a lovely book; I had it two years ago, though—and dolls are a bit young, surely?"

"Yes, I was afraid I was a bit old-fashioned and behind times. But tell me, what *would* you like, just supposing I *did* want to give you something?"

"Well, if you want to buy some little thing, I'd like an autograph book, now you've mentioned it. But if you really want to be frightfully extravagant, I'd *love* a pair of roller-skates. I know what they cost in Salisbury, because I've seen quite a decent pair there. I don't want to sound grasping, but that really *would* be marvellous, because all of us want that—especially Jackie—and we could . . . Oh, I'm sorry, it must sound as if I came here for what I could get. I'm awfully sorry. Mummie would be furious if she could hear me."

"I asked you—begged you, to tell me. Mummie would be furious with you if you were so rude as not to answer a poor old man who is ill in bed!"

"It's nice of you to put it like that," Lorrie said gratefully. "I ought to be going now."

"How did you manage to break free?"

With a smile of triumph, she told him her intricate plan of escape. He laughed quite cheerily, and she thought, as she shook hands with him, that her visit really *had* been a success, because his face had a little colour now, and his eyes were certainly more alert. He ordered the car to take her back, and with a "Have a happy holiday," let her go.

She was back in the school just one hour after

she had left it. She managed to creep up the
back stairs without meeting anyone, deposited
her outdoor things in the lobby, and made for
the dormitory. Everything was as she had left it.
She did a little hurried packing, then went back
to the common-room to "find out the worst".
But her plan had been successful. A crowd of
girls all said witheringly: "Has the little busy
bee *done* all her packing?" And she replied that
"*No*, she hadn't, but was still in the middle of
it."

"Oh no, you don't," Gay said, dragging her
back as she made for the door again. "Matron
can finish that; she'll do it a darn sight better than
you will. We're having a sing-song, and your
lovely voice (ahem!) is needed to swell the
chorus."

It was great fun, that impromptu concert.
The Fourth were there, taking their part in the
sing-song, and in the "turns" each girl was
forced to do—or pay a forfeit. Lorrie, minus a
hair slide, a stocking, and both shoes, all of which
had gone in forfeits, was suddenly told she must,
in her half-clad state, dance a folk dance all alone
up and down the corridor. She was doing it, to
the great delight of the girls, when she cannoned
backwards into the amazed Miss Heywood.
However, even that relentless woman had to

smile at the look of utter amazement on Lorrie's face as she lay on the floor at the mistress's feet!

They were allowed to stay up half an hour after the usual time, so that the concert went merrily on until half-past nine, when, after many warnings, the girls were finally shooed off to bed by Honour, Sally and June.

So this was the end of her first term, Lorrie mused, snuggling under the clothes and letting only her mouth and nose peep from beneath the blanket. With any luck, she'd have that little blue cubicle next term, and be in the Fourth with the girls she admired so much. It would be wonderful to be with June and Sally—Judy would be up too, probably, for she had certainly worked hard this term, and ought to have earned a jolly good report.

And to-morrow, by this time, she would have been home nearly five hours! Oh, the delight of Christmas at the Rectory—and of Mummie's good-night hug, and the lovely feeling of being surrounded by love, and safely back at home again.

CHAPTER XII

Home Again

The next morning, almost before it was light, the girls were awake and fidgeting to get up and get on with their packing. Gay, who was to be taken as far as Farnham and there met by her parents, was so excited that she could hardly stay in bed, and kept half getting up and then, at a warning from the rest, getting back again.

" I wish I were going home to my own people," poor Judy said pathetically. " My aunt is good to have me at all, I suppose, but I can't help feeling I'm a bit of a nuisance to her."

" How awful that must be," thought Lorrie, and said on the spur of the moment: " Why not come to the Rectory for Christmas?"

" Chiefly because I haven't been asked," laughed Judy. " I couldn't come on your invitation alone, silly, I'd have to be asked properly by your people. Besides, there seems such a crowd of you; I bet your people wouldn't want a stranger for Christmas, of all times."

Lorrie, thinking it over, felt quite certain that,

poor as they were, her family would certainly welcome a girl as lonely as Judy. She thought how selfish she had been not to have written and asked long ago. Now it seemed it was too late, and poor Judy would have a beastly Christmas.

"It's not so bad, really," Judy was saying. "We have Christmas dinner alone, but an old gentleman, a friend of my aunt's, comes in to supper. I get lovely books from my people, as a rule, so I go to bed early and read in bed. Aunt doesn't approve of reading in bed, of course, but as she's downstairs—playing chess with Colonel Walters—she doesn't know. I take some sweets up too, and have a little Christmas feast on my own."

It sounded worse than ever to Lorrie.

The journey up to London was hectic with excitement. Lorrie packed into the Third-formers' carriage, but the Fourth-formers from next door came in, and altogether they started a carol-singing session which lasted all the way from Devenham to Waterloo. People on the stations the train stopped at looked first of all in amazement, and then smiled and finally clapped! Miss Heywood, farther down the train with the remainder of the Third, put an indignant head out of the window and ordered silence. She tried hard to fight her way through the people in the corridors, but the train was packed and she had to give up. She knew it would be hopeless to give holiday tasks all round—they would simply not be done, and the new term and the new year would both begin "under a cloud".

At Waterloo Miss Heywood marshalled them together—some parents had come to Town to meet their girls, and hugs and kisses and excited laughter greeted them. The rest, Lorrie among them, walked in twos to the buffet, and had cups of tea, and then were either left to await their late "meeters", or put into taxis and taken off to their various stations and allowed to proceed. Lorrie was among these. Miss Heywood, saying loudly that she did not consider a girl of thirteen old enough to travel alone, selected a "Ladies Only" carriage, and actually put her in the care of all three occupants. Lorrie, blushing with indignation, sat sulkily in the corner and refused the well-meant efforts of the eldest lady to make conversation.

Salisbury at last! And there was Mummie— and Mary and Jackie. The train lurched to a standstill, and she bundled out with muttered thanks for "looking after me" to the three old ladies, and then she was locked in Mummie's arms, kissed enthusiastically by Mary and Jackie,

and taken out to where Dr. Green's ancient
Morris stood like some trusty steed forever at
the service of the Rectory crowd.

"Nothing," she thought, "can ever be as lovely
in all my life as this home-coming for the first
time." Everyone at first seemed amazingly polite,
but after a "high tea" the politeness wore off,
and Lorrie was the "bad boy of the family"
again. She had to recount her adventures again
and again—her feelings at the examination, her
success at the Inter-Form Match, her impressions
of all the girls, her feeling the very first day at
school!

The Rectory crowd sat round the fire in the
drawing-room—the old faded curtains drawn
against the dark night, the fire crackling merrily
in the old-fashioned grate, Lorrie on the floor,
her head against the Rector's knee and her arms
stretched out to touch Mummie on one side
and Mary on the other. Jackie curled up on
the settee, begging for more stories. Lorrie
wondered why she didn't plunge straight into
the story of her biggest adventure of all—
Basseton—but something held her back and
she didn't mention it at all.

"How dreadfully I miss Timothy," she said
at last, having tried hard not to bring sadness into the happiness of the evening. But

Home Again

Mummie said brightly: "We miss him too, but we are so thankful to hear from Honney that he grows stronger and more robust every day, that we can't grieve. He'll be home for your next holidays, my darling, and you'll be glad that you see him fit and well."

"Did you *ever* find out how and why and where all that money came from?"

Daddy said, in a rather "Rectorish" tone: "No, unfortunately we did not. I hate to feel that someone has literally saved the life of one of us, and yet will not let me thank her."

"You still think it is Miss Forsythe, don't you, darling?" Mummie said.

"Oh, it *can't* be," Lorrie said emphatically. "She might do it, but she wouldn't 'hide her light under a bushel' like this."

"I wish Prunella hadn't set herself out to make an enemy of you," Mary said thoughtfully. "I remember I was always rather frightened of her, she was so unforgiving."

"John is the one who hates her most," Jackie said, with a giggle at the thought of her brother's dislike for the Prune. "He'll be delighted when he hears they call her the Prune at school."

"John isn't to be told anything so nasty, and he certainly isn't to be encouraged to hate anyone," the Rector said firmly.

John was to arrive next day, and then the family circle, except for Tim and Honney, would be complete. Jackie said she thought there was ice on Warren's Ponds, and might they go to-morrow night—in case a thaw set in later on and they missed their chance. Mummie said she'd "see" in her "giving-in" voice. Once again it was on the tip of Lorrie's tongue to say that she might be going to have a pair of roller-skates —but she just didn't.

Up in their bedroom, later on, she decided to tell Mary and ask her advice. She felt she didn't want to tell Daddy anything that would put him in a "Rectorish" mood for the first day or two. Mary, all agog for Devenham news, listened intently to Lorrie's story—then said blankly:

"But of *course* I remember where I heard the name of Basseton before—Mummie said something about it, that first night when we had a family council about your going to school. Don't you remember?"

Yes, now she *did* remember, but she couldn't recall what it was Mummie had said. How could she have known Basseton was there, even —it was miles away from Combe Langley.

"Perhaps your Mr. Crighton was once in love with Mummie," Mary said romantically.

Home Again

" I've been reading a book rather like that."

" Oh no," Lorrie exclaimed, appalled at the idea. " Why, he's too old—he's awfully old, older than Dr. Green, I should think. The funny thing is that I can't help feeling rather worried about telling them—as if I knew, somehow, that they would be angry; but really, what *could* they be furious about? Daddy has always told us we must help when we're wanted, and I was wanted—so I went."

" Ah, well," yawned Mary, snuggling down in the little nest she always made of her bed. " I can't see that you've done wrong, except in breaking rules, and you've been doing that all your life. What I can't get over is, anyone who is ill and old *wanting* you round them, you're such a noisy person for a sick room!"

Long after Mary was asleep, Lorrie lay staring at the familiar room which in her absence had certainly become more tidy, but in big things hadn't changed at all. She gazed out through the window at her side, down on to the moonlit garden sparkling with frost. It was terribly cold outside, but snug and warm in her bed—Mummie, on her way to bed, tiptoed in and kissed Mary's sleeping form, then crept over to Lorrie. " Not asleep yet, my darling?"

" Nearly," Lorrie whispered. Now, if ever,

was the time to tell about Basseton, she thought
—but after all, why worry?

" Good night, my darling; it's lovely having
you home again."

And it was lovely being home again, Lorrie
decided, as she raced through the hard frosted
fields with the Combe Langley Guides, or made
little cakes for tea in the big kitchen, or walked
sedately to church to hear Daddy's deep " Rectorish " voice reading the lessons and delivering
his sermon. Everyone was glad to see her back,
and it did her heart good to be welcomed home
by the cottagers.

It was grand having John home too. In spite
of the Rector's words, what Lorrie thought of the
Prune had leaked out, and John, who had always
distrusted Prunella, let off steam about her, to
the intense joy of Lorrie.

But like a thundercloud that comes swiftly
across a brilliant summer sky, came Miss Graham's letter—and following it by only an hour
or so, Miss Forsythe!

The letter came on the twenty-second. They
had all been to Salisbury to do their last-minute
Christmas shopping. Mummie had had a list
" a mile long ", as Mary put it, containing all
the things she needed for the children's Christmas
tree, which was shared by the Rectory crowd and

the village children too. Lorrie had told her
parents what a dreary Christmas Judy was likely
to have, and though they had wished she had
told them before, they both thought it was much
too late to ask her down now. They decided, too,
that probably her aunt, in spite of her dreariness,
might be hurt if her niece spent Christmas
away from her. But it was decided to send her
a stocking—a nice old woollen black one—with
nuts and an orange in the toe, and all sorts of
amusing things placed in it. Lorrie had a list for
Woolworth's, and together they had tramped
miles up and down the crowded counters. But
they returned gay as larks, laden with packages,
but happy, hungry and beautifully tired.

The " crowd " went up to the Glory-hole,
where an extra substantial tea was laid. Mummie
was to have hers quietly in the drawing-room,
then they were to join forces again to pack Judy's
stocking, which positively *must* go off that night.

The noise in the Glory-hole was deafening!
So that when Nannie came in, she had to shout
to make her voice heard above the din. " Miss
Lorrie wanted in the drawing-room," she yelled.

" Anything up?" John asked as the tumult
subsided.

" I should say a lot is up, by the look of your
father's face, Master John," Nannie said omi-

nously. "It seems to me Miss Lorrie can't go anywhere or do anything without she causes a regular old up-and-downer! Never mind, my pretty," she went on, seeing Lorrie's alarmed look; "I don't suppose it's much this time, seeing you've only just come home."

"I'll bet it's my report," Lorrie said, trying not to sound worried. "I *can't* have done badly, I worked fearfully hard."

"Well, for goodness' sake go down and see," Mary said. "I hope, whatever it is, it won't put Mummie off her parcel-tying, and we must get Judy's stocking off to-night, or she won't get it in time."

Down in the drawing-room the Rector, his face rather white, was standing with his back to the fire. Mummie was sitting with a letter open on her lap. Her voice, when she spoke, sounded as if she were near to tears. Lorrie stood looking at them both in amazement. Surely, if it were the worst report in the world, they needn't look so awful!

"Lorrie, why did you not tell us that you had been to Basseton?" Mummie asked.

"I don't quite know," Lorrie said regretfully. "I knew the Head didn't approve of my going there, but I can't see why. She was quite nice to the old man herself, and I don't see——"

Home Again

"No, that is just it, you *don't* see," Daddy put in, in an almost savage voice. Lorrie looked up at his angry face—she had never known him like this before.

"And I suppose you told him your life-story, and all about Timothy's illness, and how you were at Devenham by the charity of one of my parishioners! Oh, I can't help it, Ruth!" he burst out, turning to Mummie. "I loathe all this. I will not have his words coming true, so that he can come here full of——"

"Darling, please don't speak of him like that. Now then, Lorrie, what exactly *did* you tell him?"

"I talked to him about everything at home, of course," Lorrie said, tears beginning to make her eyes blink. "I didn't know anything about it being wrong to go there the first time—and the only other time I went, he was so ill, and he sent for me, and I thought——" She was crying too much now to go on.

Mummie came to her and put a comforting arm round her shoulders and said in an anxious voice: "He was ill, did you say?"

"Yes, dreadfully ill, and he sent Salter to find me and ask me to be sure to come. What has he done wrong, Mummie? I like him. He's awfully kind when you get to know him."

"Yes, I know he is, my darling, and except

that he was unkind to Daddy, he hasn't done anything else."

"Well, it's settled one thing, Ruth," Daddy said, still in his angry hard voice. "She can't and shan't go back to Devenham. I wish to goodness I had not allowed it in the first place— I had a presentiment something like this would happen. Do you remember his words? I do— they have stayed in my memory ever since. He said, 'When you have a family of children you can neither educate nor clothe decently, you'll come to me for help,'—and now he has used this means to make me accept money to send Tim away. I'll return it, though, yes, every penny of it."

"I never knew you hated anyone, Daddy," Lorrie said, looking up at him in amazement. "I always thought you believed in forgiving everybody."

"That is enough, Lorrie. You may go to your room now, but remember this—it is dreadful to be forced to be under an obligation to someone whom you despise."

"Oh please, darling, don't say any more, I just can't bear it. Go up to the Glory-hole, Lorrie dear; I'll be up to pack Judy's stocking in a moment or two."

Lorrie walked quietly from the room. She

Home Again

knew that her mother was crying into the cushion on the settee, and that the Rector was standing, his back like a ramrod, looking angrily out into the dark garden.

Upstairs in the Glory-hole Lorrie told as much of the story as she could. She did her best to try not to cry, but the whole thing had been so unexpected and dreadful—and she had never seen her father like that before. As a rule he was so good-tempered, kindly and loving—awful to think that, underneath all that, he had such a temper and could have hated anyone so intensely as he hated Mr. Crighton.

"Well, you *must* be a muggins if you didn't ask them who this man Crighton is," John said witheringly. "That's just like you, though, Lorrie, letting a chance like that slip through your fingers. Now they'll have pulled themselves together, and they'll come up and tell us not to ask questions about things that don't concern us—if you'd asked them while the tempest was raging, they'd have said——"

"All very well for you to talk," snuffled Lorrie miserably. "How'd you like to have to leave Winchester, just because you did a spot of sick-visiting?"

"Do you honestly think Daddy means that?" Mary asked anxiously. "It does seem a dreadful shame, after you'd worked so hard all the term too."

When the others saw Mummie's face, with her eyes still red from crying and her nose obviously powdered over to disguise where her tears had flowed, their own moods became sad. Never before had the whole family felt so depressed, John declared. He stood up as his mother came in, and at the sight of her, came over and put his arms round her. "Now come along, my dear, and tell me all about it," he said in a fatherly tone. " Why has the Rector become so frightfully 'Rectorish'?"

" Oh, John darling, do you mind if we never discuss it again? I can't do anything with Daddy about it—I've tried before. It is the one sorrow I have to bear—and he has to bear it too, because it weighs on his conscience like a stone, but he won't release himself of it. I don't want to talk about it any more, dears, so let's forget it ever happened. Lorrie, pass me that tinsel, and bring the labels round this side of the table."

" Yes; but, Mummie, my lamb, you simply *must* tell me about my report. I've worked awfully hard, and now everything seems dreadful, and none of you care how I did in the exams, and I think life is *hateful!*"

" Don't cry any more, Lorrie, or you'll have

me starting again too, and we'll both have head-
aches all to-morrow. You did most awfully well,
darling, and once Daddy has got over his anger
he'll read the report to all of us."

"There he goes," John cried, peering out
through the open window down on to the dark
garden below. "Where is he going, Mummie?
Church?"

"I hope so," Mummie said seriously; then,
picking up the old black stocking, she began
filling it with the funny little presents they were
all sending to Judy. "You'll have to go into
Salisbury on your bike, John, if this is to catch
the post. Will you be safe, do you think?"

"Of *course* I shall," he said emphatically.
"I'm not your little wee laddie now, you know.
Chuck me over that gollywog, Jackie, and those
lollipops."

However much they might try to regain the
lovely Christmas spirit, they could not. Mummie
cooked some chestnuts on the shovel over the
open fire, John hung some perfectly awful
coloured chains all over the Glory-hole, Lorrie
made a specially rich brew of chocolate, but it
was all in vain—the gaiety had gone from the
house completely, and their efforts to pretend
that everything was normal only made the pathos
of it much worse. John was glad to cycle off to

post the parcel to Judy, and Mummie went thankfully downstairs as soon as she heard the Rector return. Mary and Lorrie sat over the dying fire, while Jackie went silently to bed.

"A joyful Christmas this is going to be," Mary said miserably. "I don't see how it is your fault, exactly, except if you hadn't been kept away from the picnic you wouldn't have found Basseton at all; but I do wish to goodness, old ill man or no old ill man, that you'd never seen the beastly place."

"I'm so amazed at Daddy. Honestly, Mary, you wouldn't have known him—so stern and awful, and actually letting Mummie cry all alone on the settee without going over to her. You heard what Mummie said too—she'd tried to make him get over this awful hatred before—and failed! If anyone'd told me Daddy was capable of hating anyone I'd have laughed at them. And Mr. Crighton is such a perfect old lamb, really."

"Someone is coming up," Mary said in a whisper. "If it's Daddy, I'd better leave you alone with him."

"No, you don't," Lorrie said, hanging on to her arm.

Daddy came in. It seemed to the girls that he was rather paler than usual, but his voice was unchanged as he said: " I've come to apologize to you, Lorrie, for being so beastly."

" Oh, Pops, my love, never say it," Lorrie said, throwing her arms round his neck. " I must say you gave me a shock—so altogether ' Rectorish ' and un-Dad-like."

"Yes, I was, wasn't I? I quite surprised myself! The fact is, I've a dreadful temper, and that letter roused it. I wish you had told us, when you were talking about school—then I'd have known you'd been to Basseton and it wouldn't have come as such a shock to me."

" I can't think why I didn't, except that the Head made such a fuss about it that I thought, as I'd only done what I knew you yourself would do, Daddy, that it didn't matter. I told Mary all about it, of course."

Mummie came up the stairs and entered the room softly. " Daddy says if you promise him you will never go near Basseton again, you may go back to Devenham next term. Your report is awfully good, my darling—I'm *so* proud of you—and you are to be in the Fourth next term, and you'll be able to have the little blue cubicle of your desire!"

" Well, as everything seems all right again," John said, coming in from his ride to Salisbury, " perhaps the unknown identity of Mr. Crighton can now be revealed—and the mystery cleared up for ever!"

"No, I'm sorry," the Rector said in a tone of finality. "I never want to hear his name mentioned, and I don't want this business discussed. I think the unknown sender of Tim's holiday money is known at last—I shall return the money, and the whole matter will be closed, but I want to put you all on your honour not to discuss or try to find out anything about this man or Basseton. It should be enough for you to know that I—— Darling," he said, turning to Mummie, "don't cry, please. Good night, children. Come downstairs, dearest." He led Mummie away. The children heard her saying something about it being dreadful to hear him speak of "him" like that—"as if he were a criminal, instead of the kindest . . ."

"Well, what the dickens do you make of *that*?" John asked blankly.

"Oh, for goodness' sake, let's go to bed. I've never known the house so crazy before."

"Yes, come on, Mary," Lorrie said, still grasping her report in one hand. "Good night, Pie-face," she said sweetly to John. "And thanks a million for posting the parcel to Judy."

CHAPTER XIII

Happy Ever After

Warren's Ponds were still frozen over on the morning of Christmas Eve, and the Rectory crowd, collecting a dozen or so village children, went down there to skate. Mary, in the middle of the morning, rushed back to the house and returned with an enormous jug of hot milk and some biscuits. A car drove up and stopped with a lurch near the edge of the pond. They all gathered round it, thinking that some other charitably disposèd person had brought them refreshments. Lorrie saw through the steamy glass that it was Miss Forsythe—with the Prune!

" Oh, hullo, Prunella!" she said, trying to sound delighted at the sight of her schoolfellow.

The chauffeur opened the door, and Miss Forsythe stepped out. Prunella followed and, eyeing John, said sweetly: " Oh, how lovely to see the Rectory crowd again! And still full of good works, I see. Will you allow me to join you? My aunt is on her way to the Rectory now, and we could all return there together "

"Don't be more than half an hour, then, Prunella," Miss Forsythe said, getting back into the car.

"She makes the hair stand up on my spine," John whispered to Lorrie; but Lorrie had seen the look of admiration in the Prune's eyes as she looked at John—it made Lorrie regard him from a new angle, and she suddenly realized that her "Pie-face", as she called him, had grown into an awfully good-looking boy. He looked particularly handsome just now, with his face flushed from the exercise of skating. Yes, she thought, in amazement, a girl like the Prune *would* like John for a friend.

"I'd no idea you were coming to Combe Langley for Christmas—you never mentioned it at school," Lorrie said interestedly.

"There are lots of things I don't say at school," was the reply. "How you've all grown up— I wouldn't have known you, John," she said, going over to the side where he was standing. "I knew I should find you all skating—Auntie saw you on her way back from the village. Will you fasten my skates for me, John? I never can get the straps tight enough."

"I beg your pardon," John said, bending down and fastening the straps. "There, is that all right?"

"Marvellous," she answered, in an exaggerated way which Lorrie had never heard her use.

Off she went, skating most beautifully, doing figures of eight, swaying out near the edge, swerying to the middle, graceful as a swallow.

"Golly!" said John in amazement. "I didn't know she could skate like that. I wonder if she'd teach me?"

"You bet she would," Lorrie said cattily.

She watched John skate over to where Prunella, poised like a bird for flight, stood on her toes, obviously waiting for him, yet pretending she had no idea he was near. Lorrie scowled in their direction, then joined Mary and began collecting the refreshment things.

"You needn't bother to do that," Mary said. "I'll take them back. You go and skate."

"No, thanks. I'm coming home with you," Lorrie said, trudging beside her, and carrying the jug as well as her skates. "Oh, how I'll hate that girl if she goes out of her way to be sweet to John and make him like her."

"Don't be so absurd," Mary said with a giggle. "If I know anything of John, he'll easily see through that grand manner of hers."

At home they found Miss Forsythe in the drawing-room with Daddy, looking at Lorrie's report. Mummie, seeing them coming up the path, hurried out and whispered to Lorrie: "Run and make yourself respectable, darling, then come to the drawing-room. I feel Miss Forsythe expects you to thank her for all she's done. I'm sure she means to compliment you on your report."

"I've already thanked her once," Lorrie said rather ungraciously to Mary as they made for the bathroom. "I wish anyone on earth paid my school fees except Foxie. She does expect to be lauded and honoured for it so; it's sickening."

"I'd do a lot of lauding and honouring if she'd send me to Devenham," Mary said regretfully. "You must admit now that you were wrong about not wanting to go to school. You'd hate it if you couldn't go back next term."

"Yes, I certainly would," she admitted. Certainly a little added gratitude to Miss Forsythe was called for!

But she never got the chance of giving it! No sooner had she and Mary entered the drawing-room than there was the sound of voices in the porch, then a loud sobbing and howling, and then John's voice, absolutely furious: "Oh, stop that row, you miserable little sneak."

"Don't dare to speak to me like that, after trying to drown me," came the Prune's angry wail. "Auntie, where are you?"

Happy Ever After

The entire drawing-room emptied itself on to the porch, where Prunella, soaking with pond water and smelling of weeds and mud, stood shivering in spite of John's sweater hung round her neck.

"Don't stop to talk now," Mrs. Grey said anxiously. "Lorrie, go and fill the bath—put in a whole tin of mustard too. Mary, get some hot coffee. Come here, you poor child."

But the Prune was beside herself with anger and mortification. She disregarded Mrs. Grey's entreaties and plunged into her story. "He did it purposely, Aunt. The whole family hate me— hate you too, I expect. They are all out for what they can get. Lorrie borrows money from anybody who'll lend it to her, and just because I told John so, he pushed me through the ice."

"Oh, that's not true at all!" John exclaimed indignantly. "Daddy, she was telling lies about Lorrie, and all I did was to advance towards her, and she stepped backward—she knew it was thin there—I'd already told her."

"Bath's ready," shouted Lorrie from the top of the stairs, and being unaware of what was being said, called brightly: "Come on, you poor old thing, you must be frozen."

"I'm not going to their beastly bath," sobbed Prunella. "I hate them—they'll probably try to drown me."

Lorrie's First Term

" Do pull yourself together, young lady," the Rector said in an ominously " Rectorish " tone. " I'm sorry you have had such a fright, but I really think you must control yourself now— have a bath, and afterwards apologize both to Lorrie and to John, for making unjust accusations against them."

" But are you so sure they *are* unjust, Rector?" Miss Forsythe's voice was trembling with indignation. She was a person who loved to dramatize herself, and this was just the sort of situation she revelled in. " I can't help thinking that Prunella has been badly treated, and I am sure she would not say things about Lorraine unless they were well founded."

" Well, unless you want her to die of pneumonia, I suggest you go up and put her into the bath yourself," Mrs. Grey said tersely. " We can discuss her behaviour after she has been sent home in your car, and put to bed to recover herself."

Miss Forsythe, indignation written all over her, marshalled Prunella up the stairs, leaving the Rectory crowd gaping after them.

" She's dripping all over my clean stairs," wailed Nannie furiously. " Just the same as ever, she is. I well remember there was never any peace when she used to come here for lessons.

Happy Ever After

You come into the kitchen, my poor lamb," she said, pulling at John's arm. " You're wet through yourself, and nobody seems to mind."

John was certainly fairly damp. He gazed ruefully down at his brilliant new sweater and murmured something about its being the last beastly girl he'd ever rescue.

" I am beginning to be thoroughly weary of you and your schooling, Lorrie," the Rector said bitterly. " I should like to hear what you have to say about Prunella's remark that you ' borrowed from anybody that would lend to you'. Is there any truth in that?"

" No," Lorrie said mutinously. " We went into town one day to buy Christmas presents, and I was saying to a friend of mine that I couldn't afford to buy such an expensive Mickey, when the Prune—Prunella, I mean—came forward and begged me to borrow a shilling from her. Like an ass, I did—but I paid it back on Saturday when we had our pocket-money. I've never borrowed money—it's just another lie of hers, with a grain of truth tucked away in it, and I'm jolly glad she *did* fall in."

" That's enough. Here is Miss Forsythe; you had better tell her what you have just told me."

" There is no need for her to explain," Miss

Forsythe said haughtily. "My niece is above telling untruths, Rector, and what she says I believe. I am amazed that Lorraine should have chosen such a dreadful way to repay my kindness. Prunella tells me that Lorraine has played truant on several occasions, been missing for hours together from the school, and been in disgrace with the Head and her form-mistress as well. I really must say——"

"No," interrupted the Rector coldly; "you really must say no more, Miss Forsythe. I find that Devenham has not had quite the desired effect upon Lorraine, and I should very much dislike to think that you were paying her fees in future. I must thank you for your kind intention, but there the matter will end."

"Do you mean to say you will not permit me to pay for Lorraine in future?"

"That is precisely what I mean."

"Then how will *you* manage to pay for her schooling?"

"This, I think, is something we need not go into."

Miss Forsythe began to simmer down. It gave her enormous pleasure to come and go at the Rectory whenever she liked, and to be able to play "Lady Bountiful" to them when she felt inclined. It would mean a big gap in her life if this breach between them widened, so that she felt she could not come to the Rectory.

"I think we ought to think this all over, Rector," she said more calmly. "After all, poor little Lorraine has not had the same privileges since birth that Prunella has—and so cannot quite understand the high code Devenham sets."

"Lorrie has had the privileges of a good Christian home," Mrs. Grey put in furiously. "If either of the girls is at fault, in my opinion it is Prunella, who has done her best to make trouble—and has succeeded splendidly."

"I have said my last word on the subject, Miss Forsythe," the Rector said, turning and going out of the room. Lorrie gazed after him for a moment, then said bitterly: "I wish I'd never been sent to school by you, Miss Forsythe. The Prune is a hateful, sneaking little snob, and the whole school knows it. Now she has managed to come here and spoil our Christmas—and tell lies about me and——"

"That is enough, Lorrie," Mrs. Grey said, giving her angry daughter a compassionate look. "Nobody could possibly believe that you would either borrow money, or absent yourself from school, except for very nice, kind reasons. Run up to the Glory-hole, darlings; there is a lovely fire there. Now, Miss Forsythe," she ended, as the girls went out, and they heard Miss Forsythe's voice raised to a wail of protest. On their way upstairs they passed the Prune hanging about on the stairs as if waiting for something.

"Oh, there you are," she exclaimed. "I've been waiting for you. Where's John?"

"Somewhere out of your poisonous way, I'll bet," Lorrie said curtly.

"Oh, don't make a fuss and add to the mess," the Prune said in a friendly tone. "I'm quite ready to admit I lost my temper—who wouldn't, being forced through thin ice, just because I remarked that you'd borrowed a bob from me. My stars, your brother certainly *is* a he-man!"

"Come on up, girls," came John's voice from the Glory-hole. "I'm in hiding from the sour-pippy-Prune."

It was obvious he had not heard Prunella's voice, and thought Mary and Lorrie were alone. The Prune, hearing his words, linked her arm through Lorrie's and said loudly: "You needn't be afraid of me, John; I'm better tempered now."

"Well, it's no use thinking you can suck-up to any of us now and get invited to a party, because you *can't*," John shouted back.

"Come on, Lorrie," Mary said impatiently. "Get out of here, Prunella, and don't come

back. You always did manage to make trouble
—and you're not changed a bit, in spite of your
grown-up airs and your ' privileges '."

The Prune, looking downcast, went downstairs, and they heard her enter the drawing-
room.

Up in the Glory-hole, which was hung with
John's atrocious chains of coloured paper, a big
fire burned in the grate, and having unlocked
the door for the two girls, John threw himself
down in the old armchair again. In spite of his
merry voice, his face still showed signs of anger,
and he burst out as soon as the door was closed:

"I'm fearfully sorry, Lorrie; I'm afraid I've
put paid to your career as a Devenham girl."

"No, the Prune did that. I think she always
meant to, and if she hadn't lost her temper now,
she'd have managed to make her aunt dislike me
in some sneaky way. Exactly what happened
down on the Ponds, Pie-face?"

"We were skating along — she is really
awfully good, and was showing me some fancy
stuff—when she suddenly said that it was a
shame you couldn't make your pocket-money
do, and had to be always borrowing. I said I
didn't believe you'd be such a fool; then she
said you'd borrowed from her, but she wouldn't
say anything about it, especially if she could

come to the Rectory a good deal these hols. I said I thought we'd be able to stand a bit of her, but not if she tried any blackmailing, because that was what it amounted to—you invite me to your parties and put up with me, and I'll not tell tales about you! She said a lot of nonsense about you, Lorrie, how you were given dozens of impots and so on, then she said you were always sneaking out from school—then she repeated this same rot about you borrowing, and I got fed up, so, just to frighten her, I came towards her with my head down, and simply forced her backwards—never touching her, mind you. I'd forgotten for the moment that the ice was thin just there, but I told her it was some time before. Golly, I wish you could have seen her face as it cracked and she went through!"

He went into peals of laughter.

" Oh, John, but she might have been killed!"

" No such luck. I grabbed at her and managed to haul her out. I asked her to wait while I got an old gate—you know, like they do in thrilling rescues—but she was shivering and screaming and yelling, so I just had to pull her out straight away."

" I'm afraid the Rector will be awfully 'Rectorish' about this," Mary said pessimistically. " I don't know why it is, Lorrie Grey, but any other girl could have gone to school for a term and nothing happen at all—you have to break into people's estates, and now, it seems, you have to borrow money from the very awfullest person you *could* borrow from. It's sickening."

"Oh well, let's forget it," John said, seeing Lorrie's downcast expression. "I hear both of you are to decorate the church with the Guild ladies this afternoon—as Foxie is one of the most prominent Guild members, I suggest you steer clear of her, Lorrie, my misguided one."

"Lorrie will help with the decorations as arranged," Mrs. Grey said, coming upstairs in time to hear John's speech. She put her arms round Lorrie and said comfortingly: "You won't be able to go back to Devenham, darling, but we'll do all we can to make up to you for what you have lost. None of this is your fault, whatever anyone says; you only did what any girl would do, and you've got a fine report of your work, and I'm as proud of you as a cat with two tails!"

Realizing how very deeply Lorrie was feeling the loss of Devenham, the Rectory crowd made it their business to be especially kind to her. The Rector, far from being unusually "Rectorish", was completely Daddy. He did just say at lunch-time that, for his part, he had not liked being under an obligation to Miss Forsythe, and could not help being rather glad that he was no longer in her debt. " In fact," he ended, " I shall feel that a weight has been lifted from my shoulders when I have paid her back—and paid Tim's fifty pounds back too."

Lorrie and Mary, upstairs getting ready to go to help with the decorations, had a long and serious talk about the happenings of the last few days. " If Daddy insists on paying the unknown man his fifty pounds, and then pays my school fees, where on earth will we end up, Mary?"

Mary looked serious. The Rectory crowd had always been aware of their father's financial position, and they knew now that this sudden big expense which he felt in honour bound to meet would leave him in a worse plight than ever.

" I suppose it means we'll have to economize more than ever," she said. " I'm sure I don't know how. Ah well, he is determined, so I suppose he'll manage it. It's all fearfully worrying, that's all I know."

In spite of the beauty of the decorated church —the gleaming brasses—the great sprays of berry-laden holly—the chrysanthemums and the pure gleaming light from the candles on the altar—Lorrie found her depression deepening.

Happy Ever After

Miss Forsythe, whose duties were in the Lady Chapel, went there and stayed there. The rest of the Guild concentrated on the Crib, arranged most artistically near the font. Lorrie, Mary, John and Mrs. Grey did the High Altar and the window ledges. Lorrie, slipping away from the rest, found a secluded corner behind the organ, and stood there, chin sunk in hand, thinking about the past three months—and the rather dismal future.

How foolish—childish—she had been to think that by just asking God, all her desires would be granted! The very opposite to all her wishes had happened. Once she had pictured herself setting off to Devenham with Mary—a radiant Mary whose own dreams of school had suddenly and miraculously been realized—now she saw herself back in the schoolroom with Honney, and Timothy back from his health cruise. For back he'd certainly have to come now, with Daddy determined not to accept help from whoever had sent it.

Would they miss her next term at Devenham? June Martin—would she do more than ask casually, "What's happened to Lorrie?" No, she'd probably think it a shame Lorrie hadn't returned, but having so many things to do, so many friends, June would soon forget Lorrie, whose days at Devenham had been numbered. Judy would remember, though. Yes, it was queer how she knew with such certainty that Judy would remember and be sorry.

"Day-dreaming, darling?"

"Yes, Mummie, I suppose I was," she said. "Everything seems to have gone wrong suddenly, doesn't it?"

To her surprise she saw that her mother's eyes were filled with tears. "Oh, Lorrie," she said brokenly, "I'm so dreadfully sorry, darling. I've always wanted you all to have a good start—and I thought you at least were going to have it, but Daddy is adamant about not accepting help from Miss Forsythe, and I agree with him, but, oh dear——"

"Well, darling, don't mind as much as all that. After all, I am no worse off than I was before—better in fact, because I've had one term at a big school."

"It's much more disappointing for you, having been there and having loved it so. If you'd never been, you'd never have realized what you were missing. And now Daddy is sending for Tim. . . . I feel I can't bear it if he comes home before he is really well."

"Oh, you women!" John came upon them suddenly, his hands covered with little spots of blood, where he'd been breaking holly instead of using the clippers. "Why are you so unhappy, Mums? I thought I'd caught you gossiping instead of working—I didn't know you were in tears. I've never seen so much weeping before in my life—it's a regular waterworks we're living in!"

"Stop ragging, Pie-face," Lorrie said miserably, and she repeated what her mother had just said. "I don't mind about Devenham—at least I do, but I can bear it—it's Tim that's the real worry."

"Why does Daddy feel sure it's Lorrie's Mr. Crighton that sent the boodle—cash, I mean?"

"Oh, it's sure to have been him," Mummie said ungrammatically. "But come along, let's go home, we've done all we can now, and I want to leave before the Guild people—they'd have fits if they saw me like this," she said, suddenly lapsing into her jolly manner again. "Crumpets for tea, kids, and a taster of Christmas cake."

They walked back across the dark fields, cold and frosty. The grass crackled under their feet almost as if it were stiffened with starch. Later on there would be a moon, and the whole village would look like fairyland. As a rule, on Christmas Eve they joined the choir and went round carol singing—Lorrie wondered dismally if any of them would have the heart to sing carols this year.

Suddenly John burst out: " What is wanted in this family is a little common sense and less sentiment!"

Coming upon their quiet reflections, his words seemed to break some dismal spell that had surrounded them.

Mummie laughed. " I didn't know that the Rectory crowd were unduly sentimental, darling," she said. " What I do think is wrong of us is to let silly little trivial matters worry us, and plunge us into gloom—at the time of year that should be happier than all others. Let's try to cheer up; it will be horrid for Daddy to see us return from decorating the church with faces as long as fiddles."

They did their best to be more cheerful, and only Lorrie wondered why John had spoken so decidedly.

The Rector had decided that whatever personal troubles they all had, nothing should be allowed to interfere with the usual Christmas programme. So, after an early supper, they joined the choir outside the church and went trudging off, John bearing one of the lanterns and Mary the other, to sing their carols outside the Squire's house, and from there all round the village.

John's voice, which had once been a lovely

treble, was breaking now, so that one moment he was singing like a lark, and the next " buzzing like a bee in a bottle ", as he himself put it. The Squire opened the great doors of the Hall, and allowed the lovely sounds to come in. Afterwards there was hot cocoa and buns, and all the fun of out of doors in the frost. It would have been as heavenly as ever, thought the Rectory children, if it had not been for the misery of the last few days.

Lorrie, having drunk three cups of very hot cocoa, was sitting on a seat nibbling a bun reflectively, when John came over to her and said in a whisper: " Do you think you could manage to come back with me now?"

" Back? Back where?"

" Home, you idiot!"

" But we've only just started."

" I've a confession to make. You know I went into Salisbury two days ago to post a parcel to Judy?"

" Yes," whispered Lorrie excitedly, for she knew that John's surprises were usually in the nature of a shock. But just as he was about to answer, the Rector came in, marshalled them together again, and with a cheery good night the whole party set forth for " Crannies ", a big house on the outskirts of the village.

Lorrie's First Term

So it was that Lorrie never once got the chance to talk with John again, and as he was carrying the lantern, and was rather under his father's eye, he never got the chance of slipping off home, or of confiding in Lorrie.

They were all very cold by the time the round had been completed, and Mr. Cooke, whose bass voice had boomed out through the darkness so successfully, was at last hoarse with singing. The Rector decided that the whole choir must come in for more cocoa and sandwiches. Mummie, who had already arranged for hot sausage rolls in the big warm kitchen, hurried along with the rest. As they trooped in at the back door, Nannie, looking rather pink in the face, greeted them with:

" Oh, so you are here. The rolls are just done. Bring the cocoa from the stove, please, Jackie Brown. Tom Rogers, you open the oven door and get out the rolls;" then, in an aside to Mrs. Grey, she said: " Gentleman in the drawing-room to see you and the Rector, mum."

" Oh, golly, now for it!" John whispered to Lorrie.

" Gentleman to see me at this time of night— on Christmas Eve too," the Rector said, taking off his greatcoat and hurrying off towards the drawing-room. Lorrie and Mary, exchanging glances, went after him, while Mummie followed rather hesitatingly. John, it was remembered afterwards, failed to make his appearance in the drawing-room until later!

As soon as she saw him, standing looking so fragile and pale, Lorrie said, " Mr. Crighton!" —Mummie said rather brokenly, "Daddy!" and the Rector said nothing at all.

Mr. Crighton put his arms round Mummie, kissed the top of her head, and then walked with outstretched hand towards the Rector.

" I've come to apologize, Simon," he said simply. " I was wrong and I have known I was wrong for many years—miserable, lonely, heart-aching years they have been. It isn't in your heart to refuse to forgive me now, is it?"

" No, sir, it isn't," the Rector said, taking the proffered hand in his own strong clasp. " I've nursed my grievances too long not to wish them forgotten—I've been obstinate too, and, God forgive me, I've not lived up to Christ's teaching."

The three grown-ups went over to the bright blaze of the fire—Lorrie and Mary, from the open doorway, walked discreetly backwards down the passage. Not until they had reached the kitchen did they speak one word.

" So we've got a grandfather we never knew about," Mary said in an awe-struck voice.

" He's Mummie's father. What a fool I was not to realize it," Lorrie muttered. " I *knew* I'd seen a face like his, but just couldn't place it—he's like Mummie, of course he is."

" But how did he happen to come, just now when we need him so," Mary said in a whisper, for Jackie Brown was edging nearer with a plate of sausage rolls.

The noise in the kitchen was tremendous, twenty boys and men all talking at once, and Nannie's voice raised every now and then as she gave orders to the Rectory children.

" John's at the bottom of this, I'll swear," Lorrie said with a grin. " You'll notice that the gallant Pie-face has not put in an appearance since we came home. I'll bet he's lying doggo in the Glory-hole. Come on, Mary, let's rout him out."

Sure enough, after many knockings on the locked door, John, looking rather shaken, opened to them. He had seized a store of sausage rolls on his way through the kitchen, and was sitting before the dying fire consuming them alone.

" Was it your mystery man, Lorrie?"

" It was, my pippin."

" And does it look as if there'll be a tremendous row about it?"

" We'll tell you that when you've explained,

you double-dyed villain. How — why — and when? That's what we want to know."

"Well, it's such rot, all these grown-up feuds and wars!" he said contemptuously. "It's as dead as the Dodo to keep up family quarrels. I realized that this Mr. Crighton of Lorrie's had once played the Rector a dirty trick, but as he went out of his way to be nice to Lorrie, I gathered that he was sorry now—like when we were kids and had to say 'sorry, I'll be good now'. He probably only wanted the chance to apologize, I thought. Then there was Mother—looking all white and sad, and saying the Rector would never be happy until he'd forgiven the old man, so——"

"Yes, that's it. *Do* come to the point. *What* did you do?"

"When I went to Salisbury I blued my last bob on a telephone call to Basseton. I talked to the old man himself. It was awful, really, because I only had three minutes, and he was a long time in gathering who I was and what I wanted."

"I can't think what you said," Lorrie said in admiration.

"Oh, I started off by saying I was your brother. Then I said: 'You've made an awful lot of bother down here, sir; couldn't you manage to come down and try to clear the air?' so he flustered a bit, and just then the operator said, 'Three minutes', and so I said: 'Well, good-bye, I hope we'll be seeing you,' and that was all."

"Not quite all, I fear," Lorrie said meaningly, as the sound of approaching footsteps was heard on the stairs. "Here is Fate come to make you answer for your sins."

The Rector held the door open for Mr. Crighton and Mummie. Already the old man looked better—his thin face was flushed with pleasure. He said: "Well, Lorrie, I've brought the skates."

"Oh, you old angel! Fancy you remembering," she said, flinging herself into his arms. "I *knew* we belonged. Somehow, even from that first day, I knew. We're terrifically bucked to have a grandfather, aren't we?"

John and Mary said most enthusiastically that indeed they were.

"And now, sir, what have you to say for yourself?" the Rector said to John. "This is the most flagrant case of direct disobedience and treachery we have ever had to deal with in this family."

"Oh, but, Daddy——"

"Have a heart, Pop, my sweet."

Happy Ever After

"Honestly, Daddy, he meant it for the best."

"What am I to do with them, sir?" the Rector asked, his face breaking into smiles. "I think the whole of Christmas on bread and water, don't you?"

"Well, if you want my true opinion," their grandfather said solemnly, "it is this. For many years—all their lives, in fact—you and I have robbed them of a relation! I'm not saying he was a *nice* relation! All the same, he was a grandfather, and because of my cruel temper, and your pride and obstinacy, Simon, we've stolen away from these poor children a very rich old grandfather! Now, I think a court of law would say: we must not only give back the grandfather, but also give back all the things that grandfather would have bought his grandchildren!"

"They are not to be spoilt, Father," Mummie said, looking pleased and proud of them all.

"And you don't know what you've taken on," Lorrie said warningly. "Tim's an angel, but Jackie is a rascal, as you'd have seen for yourself if she didn't have to go to bed by eight o'clock."

"I think I can cope with all the Rectory crowd," he said, with a special smile at Lorrie.

. . . .

Lorrie's First Term

It was the 20th of January, and twenty Devenham girls were talking and laughing on the platform at Waterloo Station. Mothers stood, looking cold and rather wistful—aunts, uncles and fathers were there too, but the girls were so excited at meeting again after the holidays that grown-ups were almost forgotten.

" Any sign of Lorrie Grey?" June Martin asked, of no one in particular.

" She won't be coming back," said the Prune in a pleased tone. " She was only sent on trial, sort of ' On appro.', by my aunt, you know, and as she turned out to be such a frightful dud, of course Auntie won't waste any more money on her."

" That's not true," blazed Judy Grenville. " Your aunt might have paid her school fees, but she certainly wasn't a dud, and you know it."

It was such a surprise to hear Judy speak up like that, that for a second even the Prune was silenced, but she managed to say at last: " Well, my Aunt is the best judge of that—my aunt and the Head decided she wasn't worth worrying about. Of course, if you had given *your* learned opinion it might have made a tremendous differ-ence."

" Still the same old sour Prune," June said

with a grin. " Anyway, if she isn't coming back, she isn't, and that settles it. I think it's a beastly shame—she was a jolly good sport, and she could run like a hare."

So that was all there was to it, mused Judy. It seemed strange that anyone so alive and keen as Lorrie could be so easily dismissed as that. Was it possible that she wouldn't be missed by anyone but her?

Honour came over to her and said anxiously: " Doesn't your friend Lorrie travel down by this train?"

" Apparently she isn't coming back. Prunella says she's left."

" Oh, surely not. What a pity! We could do with girls like Lorraine Grey; she was good value."

Miss Heywood came out of the waiting-room, counted heads, then boomed out in her " sergeant-major voice ": " Come this way, girls, the train is just in."

There were the usual good-byes to parents, then they all marched off to Platform 8.

Even now it seemed incredible to Judy that Lorrie wouldn't come tearing along the platform and hurl herself into the carriage beside her— but no! The train started, and there was no sign of Lorrie.

Lorrie's First Term

They had arrived at Devenham and were all marching in at the gates, when the old Rolls-Royce car that had taken Lorrie to the gates twice before drew up, and Mrs. Grey, Mr. Crighton, Lorrie and Mary got out. The look of astonishment on the Prune's face was a joy to behold.

"Oh, Judy," Lorrie cried, bounding forward. "It's so nice to see you again. Girls, this is my sister Mary."

"But I understood from Prunella that you were not coming back," Honour said, shaking Mary by the hand.

"She has a vivid imagination, our dear Prune," June said with a giggle. "How do you do?" she said, shaking hands with the entire family.

Lorrie introduced Judy, June and Sally to her people, and then, with good-bye hugs all round, she and Mary went into Devenham together with Judy.

That night, kneeling in the little blue cubicle which was hers at last, she whispered: "Do you know, God, I can't begin to thank You . . ."

PRINTED IN ROMANIA

Abbey